"Robin. You don't really know me. You shouldn't automatically trust me."

"I trusted you because I had to. You haven't disappointed me yet."

Oh, hell. That sounded like some sort of relationship had been forged between them.

Jake was relieved as much as he was on edge when he heard the sirens in the distance outside. He nodded toward the back door where they'd come in. "You stay here with the kid. I'll wait outside and show the police in."

Jake surmised the distance and direction of the approaching flashing lights. He paused for one shameless moment to admire the apple-shaped curve of Robin Carter's backside, emphasized by the clinging dampness of her wet jeans, as she bent over the bassinet, tending to her sleeping baby again.

The cops were close enough. She'd be safe.

"Thank you again, Mr. Lonergan. By the way, you never told me your first name…"

He never heard the end of her sentence. By the time she straightened from the bassinet, he was gone.

USA TODAY Bestselling Author

JULIE MILLER

ASSUMED IDENTITY

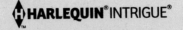

For Maggie May McGonagall Miller,
my ace writing companion and champion PR pooch.

Recycling programs
for this product may
not exist in your area.

ISBN-13: 978-0-373-69694-9

ASSUMED IDENTITY

Printed in U.S.A.

ABOUT THE AUTHOR

USA TODAY bestselling author Julie Miller attributes her passion for writing romance to all those books she read growing up. When shyness and asthma kept her from becoming the action-adventure heroine she longed to be, Julie created stories in her head to keep herself entertained. Encouragement from her family to write down the feelings and ideas she couldn't express became a love for the written word. She gets continued support from her fellow members of the Prairieland Romance Writers, where this teacher serves as the resident "grammar goddess." Inspired by the likes of Agatha Christie and Encyclopedia Brown, Julie believes the only thing better than a good mystery is a good romance.

Born and raised in Missouri, this award-winning author now lives in Nebraska with her husband, son and an assortment of spoiled pets. To contact Julie or to learn more about her books, write to P.O. Box 5162, Grand Island, NE 68802-5162 or check out her website and monthly newsletter at www.juliemiller.org.

Books by Julie Miller

HARLEQUIN INTRIGUE

*The Precinct
**The Precinct: Vice Squad
‡The Precinct: Brotherhood of the Badge
†The Precinct: SWAT
††The Precinct: Task Force

CAST OF CHARACTERS

Jake Lonergan—Is he an undercover agent who barely survived his last assignment? Or the hit man who killed the agent and assumed his identity?

Robin Carter—A successful career woman who wants to be a mother more than anything. Does she dare trust her life and her daughter's to Jake? If they survive, can she trust the mystery man with her heart?

Emma Carter—Robin's adopted daughter. Is she the real target?

Mark Riggins—The assistant manager at the Robin's Nest Floral Shop. He runs things his way when Robin's not there.

Leon Hundley—Robin's newest hire drives the delivery van…and doesn't like answering questions.

Brian Elliott—Robin's former beau is very protective.

Tania Houseman—Emma's birth mother. She survived one suicide attempt. Will she try again?

William Houseman—Tania's big brother has his sister's best interests at heart.

Hope Lockhart—Owner of the Fairy Tale Bridal Shop and Robin's friend.

The Rose Red Rapist—Is he getting careless? Or changing his M.O.?

Prologue

Jake wouldn't mind the nightmare so much if he only knew what it meant.

He thrashed in the bed, knowing he could wake himself in an instant. Instead of saving himself, however, he wrestled with the demons that had haunted his dreams on and off, from nowhere, Texas, to Kansas City, Missouri, for nearly two years now.

The violence and pain had him in their grips again, the sensations as vivid and terrifying as the images were vague and fractured—meaningless flashes of objects and people without a context. But the nightmare was the closest thing he had to a memory, the closest thing he had to understanding. So he let it steal into his bed and wash over him. He invited the torment to become a part of him.

He was hot. Sweat stung his eyes and rolled down his back. He was breathing hard, every inhale the jab of a knife in his side, every exhale a silent grunt of pain. He was hurting bad—the kind of hurt that sent men to hospitals...or the morgue.

Wheezing through the pain that seared him inside and out, he crouched behind a formless shadow in a world filled with ghosts and darkness. A voiceless command echoed in his head, forcing him to press on, demanding that he live. "You let him get away? He'll destroy every-

*thing we've worked for if he escapes. You have to stop him.
It's up to you. You're the only one who can."*

*What did the words mean? Who said them? Why did
he hurt like this? Where was he? When was he?*

What was he?

*One of the hazy apparitions moved, darting quickly
from night to night. He pulled a hunting knife from a
bag at his feet, flipped the blade into his hand as if he'd
done the dangerous maneuver a hundred times before. He
hurled the knife and the apparition sank into the darkness.*

*Another shadow rose from the swirling black mist. It
took the shape of a man, faceless and unnamed.*

*He was digging through the bag again. He didn't know
where it had come from, why he had it. It was a heavy
black satchel filled with things he couldn't see, couldn't
identify, couldn't remember. That's when he saw the gun
in his hand. It was a wicked, streamlined thing of black
steel that felt comfortable there, like it was a part of him.
Its shiny surface gleamed in the shadows. He knew that
gun better than he knew his own name.*

*He squeezed the trigger and the shadow jerked. But
it didn't fall. He couldn't see a face, but he could see the
gun, pointed at him, and he dove for the ground at the
flashes of gunshots exploding in the night.*

*All Jake knew was the driving need to hunt down prey
that was getting away. The instinct to run cramped his
sore, weary muscles. But somehow he knew he belonged
to the darkness. He had to hide. And wait. And kill.*

*The barrage of deafening noise came next. Explosions.
Thunder. The sounds pierced the darkness, filled it up.
Guns and bombs and pain and death. He was stuck in the
middle of it. Or maybe he was the cause of it.*

"You have to stop him."

He was stalking the faceless shadow. He was the bringer of death.

The nightmare took a surreal turn as snow began to fall in the darkness. He was hotter than he'd ever been, and it was snowing—but not light, airy flakes. White, acrid pellets stung his nose, melted against his skin, branded him.

The walls were collapsing around him. He needed to get out of there. Now.

But he needed to get the job done even more.

He slung the bag over his burning shoulder and pushed to his feet. Crouching low, he hurried through the darkness, snatching his knife from the dead man's chest and tucking it into his belt before he flattened his back against a crumpling wall and peered around its black edge into the fire-studded darkness.

He blinked away the snow and sweat and pain, and stilled his breath. There. He spotted the limping shadow and moved from his hiding place. Victory was his. He lined up his prey in the crosshairs of his gun. Jake squeezed the trigger.

A searing pain exploded in his shoulder and he staggered back. A crimson stain added color to the nightmare. The bag dropped to his feet. He clutched his arm to his side and cursed the numbness creeping down to his fingertips.

"You have to stop him."

He raised his gun again.

There was blood in his eyes now. Red was everywhere he could see. The noise was so loud he couldn't hear his own thoughts. The very air tasted of sulfur.

He was running out of time. Kill or die.

He squeezed the trigger.

Fire ripped through his skull. Pain consumed him. He was falling, plummeting toward death.

For one blink, there was clarity, understanding.

But the blackness rushed up from Jake's feet and swallowed him whole, taking a clear image of the man's face, of his surroundings—of freedom from this nightmare—with it.

Jake came awake on a groan and jackknifed upright in the bed. The sheet and blanket were twisted around his legs. His naked skin glistened with cold beads of sweat in the dampish night air. His chest heaved in and out on deep, ragged breaths as he oriented himself to his surroundings.

He eased open his fists, releasing the pillow he'd crushed, flexing his long fingers against the gray light that filtered into the studio apartment from the street lamp outside his window, verifying that he held neither gun nor knife. The deafening fusillade that had filled his ears a moment earlier faded into the lazy drumbeat of thunder and the soft patter of raindrops on the sidewalk and street below.

Jake turned his face to the screen at the half-open window and breathed in slowly, deeply—noting each fresh, tangible detail of the world around him. His waking world was still dark, but the rain brought a calming sound and the scent of ozone into his room. The springtime temperature cooled his heated skin.

Kicking his covers to the foot of the fold-out bed, he swung his legs over the side and planted his feet on the solid familiarity of worn wood and a discount store throw rug.

Wearing nothing but the boxer shorts he slept in, Jake rose and crossed to the apartment's lone closet and opened the door. He pushed aside the hangers that held a handful of jeans and shirts and reached behind them to pull out a worn, black leather bag. Its heavy weight was the lone anchor to a past he couldn't remember, the one tangible reality from the nightmare he couldn't forget.

With an easy clench of muscle he lifted the bag and dropped it onto the bed. Pulling apart the singed handles, he dug into an inside pocket and pulled out a badge. The nickel and brass were shiny beneath his touch as he rubbed his thumb over the letters and numbers he'd traced so many nights before.

Drug Enforcement Agency. J. Lonergan.

But it meant nothing to him. Not the badge, not the name.

He reached into the same pocket and pulled out three different sets of passports and ID cards. Three different identities, three different home addresses, three different versions of the same grim face staring back at him. None of them stirred a glimmer of recognition, either. What kind of man needed three aliases? Why would he have taken so many trips to Central and South America? He felt no ties to the DEA—no ties to Houston, St. Louis or Chicago, either. He felt nothing but confusion. The badge might be his. But it could just as easily have been taken off one of the faceless shadows he killed every night in his dreams.

Which one of these names was real? Were any of them?

He scraped his palm over the craggy ridges and hollows of his battered nose and grizzled jaw and cursed. Why couldn't he remember? Why the hell couldn't he remember anything before that morning he'd woken up in a tiny Texas border-town hospital?

Was he a cop who'd nearly died in the line of duty? Or the man who'd killed a cop and assumed his identity?

After two years, with no one coming to the hospital to check on him, and no image that matched his face on any television screen in any of the towns he'd lived in between then and now that even *felt* familiar, he was beginning to believe it had to be the latter. He was a cold-blooded killer without any memory of the monster he'd once been.

He tossed the badge and passports back into the bag. The nightmare wouldn't come back tonight. But neither would sleep. The blank holes and black walls in Jake's memory—Jake, because he had no idea what the *J* on that badge stood for—disturbed him more than the violent images in between.

Some nights he took a cold shower. Other nights he bench-pressed the weights in the corner of the room until his strength was spent. On the worst nights he poured shots of tequila to erase the sweat from his skin and numb the emptiness in his head. Tonight, the rain and a long walk would do.

Without turning on the light, Jake quickly dressed in jeans, a T-shirt and work boots. Before putting away the bag, he pulled out a gun and ankle holster and strapped it to his leg. He slipped a hunting knife from beneath his pillow, flipped it with practiced ease in his hand and tucked it into the leather sheath inside his boot.

He couldn't remember his own name, but he knew how to wake himself from a nightmare without crying out and alerting his enemies—not that he knew who those enemies might be. He knew how to arm himself before walking out into the shabby side of downtown Kansas City after the sun had set and every reputable business had closed for the night. He knew how to survive in the shadows of society without calling unwanted attention to himself.

But he didn't know how to remember.

Needing something physical, something familiar, something as rooted in the present moment as he could make it to silence the demons from his forgotten past, Jake set the satchel back into the closet, locked his door and disappeared into the stormy night.

Chapter One

"I know it's late, Emma. But try to help Mommy just a little bit longer. Just one little belch. Please?" Of all the evenings to outgrow her night-owl schedule, Robin Carter's infant daughter had decided that the one night her mother wanted to stay up late she would be a fussy pants.

Hiding her frown of frustration, Robin shifted the precious weight in her arms to gaze down into drowsy eyes that were fighting hard not to sleep, despite a full tummy and the midnight hour. From the moment she'd first met her infant daughter, barely two months ago, those blue eyes had been irresistible. Robin glanced over at the clock on her office desk, then back to the baby's agitated plea. They were still impossible to resist.

"You're right. We'll figure out how to make the books balance in the morning. Right now we'd better get home to our comfy beds." She put Emma back to her shoulder and patted her soft back until she heard the burp. Robin grinned, reassured and reenergized by the healthy sound. "Dainty and delicate and tough as a Marine, aren't you?"

Despite the difficult circumstances surrounding Emma's birth, and the adoption that had changed both their lives, Emma did everything in a healthy, robust way. Burping. Eating. Crying. Growing silky brown hair. Claiming her new mother's heart. The four-month-old was all Robin had wanted but feared she would never have.

Relationships had failed.

In vitro had failed.

Robin was closer to forty than to thirty now. She'd put herself through college on scholarships and hard work, built her own floral design business, invested smartly, bought a house with an acreage just outside of Kansas City and landscaped and remodeled it to become her dream home. But her dream could never really be complete if she was all alone.

With her biological clock ticking like mad and no man she wanted in her life, Robin had listened to the advice of her attorney and gotten on a waiting list to obtain the one thing she hadn't been able to achieve on her own—a beautiful, healthy baby. Adopting Emma was a miracle that had altered Robin's lonely, workaholic life in wonderful ways she was discovering each and every day as the two of them became a family.

Normally, Emma adapted to wherever Robin took her—errands, shopping, visits with friends. She especially liked coming to work at the Robin's Nest Floral Shop, napping in the bassinet in the corner of Robin's quiet office or supervising customer satisfaction and employee workloads from the baby sling Robin often wore across her chest. Maybe Emma loved the shop because of the building's cool, climate-controlled air, or the friendly employees who doted on her. Or maybe Emma simply loved being close to the reliable, down-to-earth practicality and unconditional love that Robin provided.

But tonight was not *normal*. And Emma was not a happy camper.

Neither was Robin.

The baby's restlessness could be attributed to something concrete, like the changing barometric pressure as the spring storm gathered strength outside. But it was more likely that Emma had picked up on Robin's frustration with the numbers on her computer. Perhaps Emma was being fussy because Robin had been fussing over the business's books ever since the shop had closed three hours earlier. Her accountant had had some questions about discrepancies between receipts and job estimates and stock manifests. Robin had been away from work far too much since Emma's arrival, and maybe her employees had gotten lazy about keeping track of everything. But spending the night in her office wasn't going to make the books balance for her. And although Emma normally stayed up past eleven most nights, she didn't want her daughter thinking the shop and office were her new home, either.

Robin lay Emma in the bassinet and leaned over to kiss her dimpled cheek, taking a moment to inhale the innocent fragrance that was all powder and baby wash and Emma herself. "Let Mommy make one more check around the place and then we'll go home."

She pulled the cotton blanket over her round little body, hoping that second bottle of formula, a clean diaper and the muffled rhythm of the rain and thunder would soothe her to sleep. But when Emma's face squinched up, promising another bout of crying, Robin hardened her heart against the urge to take the baby into her arms again. "Give me five minutes and we'll be out of here."

Emma's tiny fists batted the air. Robin touched one of the perfect little hands and guided the baby's thumb into her mouth. Emma started sucking and quieted for a few moments, but Robin had pushed them both long enough for one day. The bookkeeping questions could wait for tomorrow. Her daughter came first.

Turning away before sympathetic tears stung her own eyes, Robin quickly shut down her computer and stuffed the shipping manifests and customer orders into their respective files. Since she'd started carrying the diaper bag, her brief case and purse spent most of their time locked up in her car. She carried the necessities in her pockets or, like these files, tucked them into the flowered backpack that was Emma's diaper bag. Pulling her keys from the pocket of her jeans, she hurried out into the hallway and closed the door quietly behind her.

Although she'd always been cautious about her safety whenever she worked late at the shop, Robin had become doubly paranoid lately, and moved through the building to recheck the locks on the back loading bay doors, the windows in the stock and workrooms, the massive walk-in refrigerator where fresh flowers were stored, as well as the doors at the front of the Robin's Nest Floral Shop. It wasn't just that bone-deep need to make sure her child was safe, whether she brought Emma to work or stayed at home with her. A friend and employee of Robin's had been abducted from this very neighborhood eight months earlier. Janie Harrison had been raped and murdered, and her abductor, believed to be the Rose Red Rapist, was still at large.

Robin hated the nickname the press had given to the serial rapist. They'd latched on to the colorful appellation because his first victim had been abducted outside the Fairy Tale Bridal Shop across the street. Rose Red, like the fairy tale, instead of simply naming him after the flower he left with his victims after each brutal attack. At one point, KCPD had even suspected the creep had gotten the roses at her shop.

So Robin didn't stock red roses anymore. If a bride or some other client wanted the red flowers for a wedding or funeral, then she'd special order them. It made her sick to think she'd enabled the creep in even that small way.

Confident that every lock was secure, Robin peeked through the front windows into the wet night outside. Thick sheets of rain puddled on the pavement and created a translucent curtain that dimmed the street lamps and the occasional headlights from vehicles that drove past. Normally, she loved the rain. It made her lawn green up, and the irises she'd planted last fall around her house and in the window boxes in front of her shop were blooming like crazy. The world outside her business near downtown Kansas City seemed gray and quiet tonight—perfect for sleeping or curling up with a good book or rocking a tired infant to sleep.

But the women of Kansas City lived in fear on nights like this, wondering what danger might lurk in the shadows. Robin was no exception. The Rose Red Rapist reportedly came out of nowhere, striking his victim from behind and hauling the woman away in a white van to some unknown location where he assaulted her before bringing her back and dumping her body in this refurbished uptown neighborhood.

As if to emphasize the danger, a bolt of lightning zapped across the sky and a crack of thunder split the air, startling Robin and instantly pricking the hairs beneath the sleeves of the blue oxford blouse she wore. She crossed her arms and inhaled deeply, fighting off the chill that seemed to creep right through the glass to raise goose bumps on her skin.

As her eyes readjusted to the darkness, Robin detected a subtle movement in the shadows across the street. She braced one hand against the cool, damp glass and leaned closer, squinting to bring the lone figure, with shoulders hunched against the rain, into focus. Lightning flashed again and Robin caught a glimpse of the slender figure darting beneath the awning above the front entrance to the bridal shop. A coat or dress swung around the shadow's knees.

A woman. Alone on a night like this. Robin's heart knotted with concern. "Oh, sweetie. Be safe."

The woman pulled a hand from her pocket and brushed her straight, wet hair off her pale face. Then she lifted her head and looked straight at Robin. Maybe. The shop was dark and the nearest streetlight was farther down near the parking lot entrance. Robin should be nothing more than a shadow herself.

But the young woman's dark eyes never seemed to blink. She stared so hard that she must be seeing Robin watching her.

Robin breathed one moment of uncomfortable trepidation beneath the imagined scrutiny. In the next breath, she considered unlocking the front door and inviting the stranded woman inside the shop where she'd be warm and safe. Robin moved to the front door, pulled the keys from her pocket. Then the lightning flashed again.

But when Robin blinked her eyes back into focus in the darkness, the young woman was gone.

"Where…?" The woman must have found enough respite to gather her courage and run off in the rain and shadows to her destination again. "Be safe," Robin whispered again.

She needed to do the same. Robin shook off her apprehension about her books, the stormy weather and those mysterious shadows outside and returned to her office. "I'm back, sweetie."

She was greeted by a soft suckling sound that gave her hope that a ride in the car would coax Emma into a deep sleep that would last for five or six hours—long enough to get a decent rest herself so she could tackle the problems at work with a fresh eye in the morning. Smiling at her daughter's resilience, Robin picked her up from the bassinet and strapped her into her carrier. She thanked Emma for her patience with a gentle kiss to her forehead and then slipped a yellow knit cap over her hair and covered her with the blanket. Certain her daughter was warm and secure, Robin pulled the cloth protector over the carrier and closed the round viewing vent over Emma's face to shield her from the rain.

Before turning out the lights, Robin pulled on her yellow raincoat, slipped the diaper bag over her shoulders and picked up Emma's carrier. Since she'd put away her pepper spray two months earlier, not wanting to risk any accidental contact with her baby's delicate skin, Robin pulled a security whistle from the pocket of her slicker and looped the lanyard around her neck. Then they were moving through the familiar hallway and workrooms to the employee entrance from the parking lot beside the restored redbrick building.

With the steel door locked solidly behind her, Robin waited a moment beneath the green-and-white-striped awning above the entrance, assessing her surroundings. Pulses of lightning lit up the clouds in the skies overhead, giving her brief flashes of the rain and night around her.

Although the small lot was well lit, the emptiness between the brick walls of her building and the next one on the opposite side of the lot hitched up her apprehension a bit. Besides the shop's delivery van, parked near the alley behind the building at the end of the loading dock, the only car left was hers, parked in a circle of light beneath the lamppost nearest the street. Lights were working; doors were locked. Street-level shops were closed and the storm seemed to have driven any tenants who lived on the upper floors of the neighborhood high-rises inside.

Still, the rain hitting the awning over her head and rhythmic rumbles of thunder drowned out any telltale sounds that would alert her to approaching footsteps on the sidewalk or to vehicles passing on the street. She knew that, despite all her precautions, there was an inherent danger to a woman walking to her vehicle alone at night in the city. It required a deep, fortifying breath and the knowledge that she had a child to protect from the elements for Robin to pull her hood up over her chin-length hair, stick the whistle in her mouth and step out into the rain.

With her head slightly bowed against the rain drumming on her slicker, Robin hurried across the lot. Hugging Emma's carrier in the crook of her elbow, she made sure there was no one hiding beneath or around her car before tapping the remote and unlocking the doors.

As challenging as it had been at first to learn all the buckles and straps and tabs and slots of loading Emma into her car seat, Robin now made quick work of opening the back door and sliding the carrier into place. Once everything had locked and the car seat was secure, she spit the whistle from her mouth and leaned inside to open the vent on Emma's pink carrier cover, hoping to find a sleeping baby inside.

Instead, blue eyes stared up at her. With her darling face crinkled up with displeasure and looking as if the tears were about to let loose again, Emma swung her tiny fists in the air. "Oh, sweetie. Just give up the fight and go to sleep."

After wiping her wet fingers on the leg of her jeans, Robin reached beneath the damp material that had kept Emma dry and guided a thumb back to Emma's mouth, earning what Robin interpreted as a resigned whimper that things were okay. For now. "You'll be just fine in a minute, sweetie. I promise." She straightened Emma's cap, cupped her soft cheek and smiled. "Mommy loves you."

A flicker of movement reflected off the back window. Startled by the darting shadow, Emma grabbed for her whistle.

Before she could blow it, something hard smacked her across the back, throwing her against the frame of the car with bruising force. She thought the wind had slammed the door against her. But just as it registered that the rain was falling in a straight curtain around her car, she was struck again. This time, lower down. Something hard, narrow and unforgiving cracked against the back of her knees, toppling her to the pavement.

Robin screamed as another blow slammed across her back. Her palms scraped over the wet asphalt as she spread-eagled on her stomach, the wind knocked from her chest. As the pain radiated through her legs, and she struggled to inhale through her bruised lungs, she realized the baby backpack she wore had probably saved her from a crippling or killing blow.

The same backpack also served as an easy handle for her attacker. He latched on to the straps and dragged her several feet away from the car. Terror poured into her veins, thrusting aside the shock that had addled her thoughts. This was it. She was about to become the Rose Red Rapist's latest victim. She needed to shake off this oxygen-deprived stupor, ignore the pain and fight. She had a child to live for and protect.

Her world spinning, her lungs burning, her legs wobbly as a toddler's as she pushed up onto her hands and knees, Robin quickly realized three things. Her attacker's hands weren't on her anymore. She squinted against the strobing effect of the lightning flashes overhead to see that he had stepped over her prone body and was rifling through the contents of her car. Her attacker was dressed in black from head to toe. There was no face, no hair color to see and identify. And he carried a baseball bat in one gloved hand.

Clarity seeped into her brain with every breath, each one stronger and deeper than the last. Maybe this wasn't a rape. Maybe he wanted her purse. Or it could be a carjacking. And that meant…Robin staggered to her feet and lurched toward the figure in black. "Get away from my baby!"

She stuck the whistle between her lips and blew. The shrill alarm pierced the air. She blew it again as she lunged for the arm with the bat. Robin got her hands on his wrist as he whirled around. She banged it against the fender of her car, trying to shake the weapon loose.

Despite her assailant's muffled curse, he quickly regained the upper hand, spinning Robin to one side. With her arms up to struggle with the bat, she left her body exposed and her attacker seized the advantage, ramming his fist into her already sore ribs, doubling her over and robbing her of breath. Robin's grip on the man loosened and he easily pulled away, raising the bat. He grunted with the effort of his swing as he brought it down toward Robin's head.

She ducked to the side, saving her life as the bat crashed into the top of her trunk, denting the metal hard enough that the blow must have tingled through her attacker's arms and hands. He hesitated a moment, flexing his fingers, and Robin slipped away and reached into the car for Emma. "Come on, sweetie."

Before she could release the latch to remove the carrier from the car seat, she was struck again. She absorbed another blow to the backpack that drove her to the ground.

"Stay down!" her attacker whispered on an angry curse.

Yet, almost as soon as he'd issued the order, he was hauling her up to her knees.

"Take my purse. Take my car. Take whatever you want," she begged, slapping at his gloved hands and struggling to get to her feet. "Just let me get my baby!"

"Shut up." Huffing and puffing from the exertion of the attack, the man fisted his hand around the straps of Robin's backpack and dragged her across the parking lot. This was more than getting her out of his way this time. He was hauling her to the alley behind the shop, around the far side of the loading dock, hiding them from any view from the parking lot, much less the street.

With her hood long gone, the rain splashed in her face, reviving her will to fight. "Let go of me!" Robin clawed at his grip. She twisted and kicked. "Please," she begged. "I just want to save my baby."

"Shut up!" He dropped her behind the delivery van, glanced up and down the alley as though making sure they were all alone. "I gotta do this."

Cold, stark terror swept through Robin like the rain soaking into her clothes. She smacked at his hands as he ripped open her jacket and unhooked the belt at her waist. "Stop!"

He popped the buttons on her blouse and unzipped her jeans. The cold rain hit her stomach, soaked into her panties. Robin thrashed and clawed at him. She was in mortal danger, about to become the next victim of the Rose Red Rapist.

And her baby was all alone. Abandoned once more. Helpless, without a mother. Alone at night in the rain.

"Please. I have a child—"

"Quit fightin' me." He cuffed her across the face, stunning her. He rose to his feet and straddled her. "You want it this way? Then this is how we'll do it." As the man raised the bat, Robin kicked out, aiming for that most vulnerable part of his anatomy.

But the man was quicker. The bat switched its target, swinging into her calf and deflecting her blow.

But the bruising strike didn't stop her. Ignoring the pain, Robin rolled into the man's legs, knocking him back against the side of the van. With one swift, jerky movement she got to her feet and limped around the bumper of the van toward freedom.

"Emma?" Robin gasped the word on a determined breath.

But bruised and battered, she was no match for the stronger man. She never saw the bat this time. She only knew the stinging blow that caught her at the juncture of her shoulder and neck, spinning the world out of focus and knocking her to the asphalt.

This time, he grabbed her by the ankle and dragged her back to his killing place. He flipped her onto her back and stood over her. The stocking mask he wore obscured his face, but she had no doubt about the hateful displeasure in his voice. "Is this the way you want it?"

Robin got up onto her elbows and tried to scoot away. "I won't leave my baby."

But he followed. Shaking his head, he closed the distance between them. Her back hit the concrete wall of the loading dock and she knew there was nowhere left to run.

"This ends now." The bat swung up again and Robin braced for the blow.

But it never came.

A white-haired ghost materialized from the rain with a guttural roar. Strong hands closed around the bat, wrenching the weapon from her attacker's grip.

The bat skittered away into the darkness as the ghost lifted her attacker off his feet. Her mysterious rescuer wrapped a meaty forearm around her assailant's neck and carried him off into the shadows. The attacker's body went limp and her savior tossed him aside into the alley.

Robin grabbed hold of the wall behind her to push herself to her feet. But her knees buckled and her world blurred as the ghost's craggy, disfigured face came into view in the light above the loading dock. He was real. Big. Frightening. He growled something her stopped-up ears couldn't make out and lunged for her.

Icy blue eyes and her own scream were the last things Robin remembered as her world faded to black.

Chapter Two

"Lady? Lady!" Jake caught the woman before her head hit the pavement. Nothing like a scream of terror to make a man feel every inch the monster his nightmares purported him to be. Still, he adjusted the woman in his arms as gently as he could, then laid her on the wet asphalt. "You're welcome."

He squatted down beside her, trying to block some of the rain that hit her face, looking her over from head to toe. She was long and lean and pale as milk. The backpack she wore was soaked and stained from her struggles, but he lifted her slightly to pull the squishy pack beneath her neck to cushion her head. He snapped her jeans closed and pulled her raincoat together to cover her body. Thank God the bastard hadn't completed what he'd started. Didn't mean he hadn't done some damage. Jake pushed aside the collar of her blouse. Carefully avoiding the puffy red-and-violet welt across her collar bone, he pressed two fingers to the base of her throat. Her skin was creamy soft, chilled by the rain. But she had a pulse. The scuffed-up raincoat was moving up and down, too, so she was breathing.

She just wasn't awake.

He sifted his fingers through her wet brown hair, moving the heavy waves from side to side to check her scalp for any contusions that could explain her unresponsive state. Nothing but silky hair. Jake pulled his hand away, feeling a little guilty that his fingers had warmed and lingered, mistakenly thinking the first-aid check had felt like some kind of caress. He knew how to nip that sensation in the bud. Remember the scream. Forget the niceties. He gave her cheek a couple of gentle smacks. "Come on, lady. Open your eyes."

He heard a moan behind him in the alley and Jake turned, springing to his feet. His gaze zeroed in on the loser with the mask who had the idiot idea he was coming back for round two. Jake almost felt sorry for the guy. The woman's attacker had the skills of an amateur. He'd probably subdued the woman with an initial blitz attack. But he was out of his league going up against someone who could fight back. Even now, he was already advancing before he had his balance centered over his feet.

And then Mr. Amateur had the bright idea to pull a knife. The thin steel blade gleamed in the next flash of lightning. He choked out a breathy warning. "This isn't about you."

Jake glanced down at the woman behind him, lying still and vulnerable at his feet. Decision made. Without taking his eyes off the approaching threat, Jake pulled the hunting knife from his boot, flipping the weapon in his hand to warn the guy he knew how to use it. "It is now."

That's right. Mine's bigger than yours, he taunted silently, watching the eyes go wide behind the stocking mask.

Just then a cat howled across the parking lot, and the attacker's head jerked toward the interruption. Although the mewling was muted by the rain and thunder, Jake tuned his ears to the sound, as well, wondering if the guy was that easily distracted or if he needed to be on guard against some other threat. A quick glance revealed little except darkness, rain and the empty street beyond the parking lot.

Whatever had spooked the guy was evident in the rapid rise and fall of his shoulders as his breathing quickened. Or maybe he was finally wising up to the idea he wasn't getting past Jake. With one last heave of breath, the shadowy figure cursed. "You should have minded your own business."

And with that, he turned tail toward the opposite end of the alley.

The instinct to run after him jolted through Jake's legs, but he stayed rooted to the spot. The woman was still down, out cold and completely unprotected. He needed to stay here. Besides, what the little creep lacked in skills, he made up for in speed, and Jake would have a hard time catching him.

What could he do when he caught the guy, anyway? It wasn't like he could arrest the pervert. And though Jake had intimidation down to a science, outside of the bar where he sometimes had to show a rowdy customer the door, he preferred to keep his skills on the down-low. Calling attention to himself with the police or anyone else wasn't something he could afford to do until he figured out whether he was the law, or running from it. Besides, the unconscious woman had to be his priority.

Once the figure in black had darted around the corner out of sight, Jake risked turning to the woman again. He tucked his knife back into its sheath and knelt down to test the chill on her wet cheeks. He could feel her warm breath, but she didn't even flinch at his unfamiliar touch.

"Ma'am?" He hadn't felt any bumps on her head. Did she have internal injuries? Was this shock? A blow to the carotid artery could interrupt blood flow to the brain, and that bruising welt was placed in about the right spot to make that happen.

Jake swore. How the hell did he know things like that?

He tapped her cheek again. "Come on, lady."

He glanced over his shoulder at the squeal of tires on wet pavement in the distance. Was the little creep really that fast? Or did he have an accomplice waiting for him to make a quick getaway? What had they wanted with this woman? And how many men did they think it took to subdue a skinny slip of a thing like this, anyway?

Lightning flashed in the clouds overhead and a bad feeling crawled across Jake's skin. The violence surrounding this woman didn't feel random. An attacker and an accomplice sounded planned.

All the more reason to get her up and out of here.

He glanced down at the sleeping beauty. Despite the scrape along her jaw and the wet hair that clung to her forehead and cheeks, trailing sooty rivulets across her skin, she was stirring something more than concern and worry inside him. Being attracted to an unconscious woman couldn't be a good thing. With his life in the state of flux it was, it wasn't a good thing to be attracted to anyone. Angry at the damn hormones and feelings brewing inside him tonight, Jake swiped the water off his own stubbled face.

That's when he got the idea to cup his hands to catch the rain. While he waited for his palms to fill, Jake thought about what had brought him to this spot in the first place, playing nursemaid to an injured woman.

He'd heard a scream on his late-night walk. He'd heard a lot of screams in his lifetime. He wasn't sure how or why he knew that, but he knew the sounds of a woman in distress had always gotten under his skin and somehow gotten him into trouble.

For a few seconds, he'd considered ignoring it. Maybe he could report it anonymously when he got back to his apartment. He had too many problems of his own to get involved in somebody else's trouble. But then he'd heard the whistle. Over and over. He'd heard the panic in that shrill sound piercing the rain and an alarm had gone off inside him.

Maybe he'd been itching for a fight, something to expel the frustrated energy that consumed him. Maybe it was the bar bouncer in him, trained to neutralize any ruckus before it got started. But when he'd cut through the alley behind the buildings to answer that alarm, he'd seen that loser dragging the woman out of sight behind the van— going after her with a baseball bat. Something inside Jake had snapped. The woman was in danger, and something in his DNA that he couldn't remember had been compelled to save her.

Pity that beating down a man with his bare hands came to him a lot easier than waking a sleeping woman.

With the rainwater overflowing his palms, Jake pulled back and tossed it on her face.

Her eyes instantly shot open and she sputtered. Her hands fisted on the pavement and she shook her head, flinging more water onto his boots. She blinked, focused, caught sight of him and immediately shrank away with a choking huff of fear. Even as he held his hands up in surrender, showing he meant her no harm, she was cowering away from him, scrambling to sit up. He reached out one hand to help her and she scooted away on her bottom, until her back hit the wall of the loading dock.

"Get away from me!" she rasped, her voice tight with fear.

Could be an instinctive reaction to finding a man kneeling over her after fighting off that coward who'd assaulted her. Could be she'd just got a good look at his harsh, beat-up face.

The reaction in those suspicious gray-blue eyes was enough to sour any attraction he might feel.

"I'm not going to hurt you."

But she wasn't buying it. No way. She pushed her hair out of her eyes to really size him up. If anything, the woman breathed harder, went even paler as she calculated his strength and the size of his fists. She was probably wondering how he'd gotten the scars and if he was as violent a man as he looked.

He knew the military cut of his prematurely gray hair didn't leave any handsome possibilities to the imagination. The face and bulk and no-nonsense demeanor created an intimidating combination that made his job as a bouncer/bartender an easy gig. They got the job done, too, when it came to keeping his friends few and strangers who asked questions he didn't want to answer even fewer. The ugly mug was who he was. It had probably served him well in his former life—kept people from messin' with him.

Although it played hell when he was trying to convince a frightened woman he meant her no harm. "I'm not the man who hurt you."

She surprised him completely when she jerked her head in a nod. "I know. You're bigger than he is. He was dressed in black from head to toe. You…startled me. That's all."

Startled was putting it kindly. But at least she was thinking rationally. Probably no injury to the head, then. Cautiously, Jake pushed to his feet. Big mistake. Now he was towering over her. She visibly cringed. But six feet two inches of muscle, scars and a broken face wasn't something he could change. He held his arms out to either side and kicked the ball bat over to her, giving her the option of arming herself against him if it made her feel safer.

Not that he still couldn't overpower her if he had to.

She knew it, too. Smart woman. With a determined tilt to her chin, she braced her hands on the wall behind her and staggered to her feet, ignoring the bat. "Please. I have a child. I need to get to her."

Jake shook his head. They were alone in this alley now. "I didn't see any kid."

"You didn't…? Emma?" She straightened against the concrete wall and looked beyond the van. "She's over there. He pulled me from my car."

Jake glanced behind him. Ah, hell. That explained the wailing he'd heard. It was the kid, crying, not a cat. "Is that your car?"

She nodded. "I need to get…" She took two steps before her right leg buckled and she fell back against the loading dock.

Jake darted forward, catching her by the arms to help her stay on her feet.

"Don't touch me." She instinctively reached out to push him away. But just as quickly, her fingers curled into the front of his shirt. He felt the unsteady tug on his skin all the way down to his bones. "Apparently, I need your help. So I'm deciding not to be afraid of you." She actually pointed a warning finger at him. "Don't make me regret that."

At that brave statement, the corner of his mouth hitched up into an admiring grin and Jake adjusted his grip to firmly cup her elbow. "No, ma'am."

"You know, you're not as scary when you smile." *As scary*. Interesting distinction. The woman was smart *and* honest. She brushed the water from her face and gifted him with a smile of her own. "Thank you for saving my life, Mr.…?"

"Lonergan."

"Thank you for saving me, Mr. Lonergan." She tried to adjust the backpack on her shoulders, but winced in pain and nearly doubled over. "Ow—"

"Easy."

She braced her hand against his chest and fell into him, hanging on as his arm snaked behind her waist to give her the balance she needed. "I do need your help, don't I."

The lightning overhead illuminated her face for a split second. Her lips pinched thin against whatever pain or dizziness she was fighting.

While he waited, Jake asked, "What's your name, brave lady?"

"Robin." She sucked in an easier breath, and then another. "Robin Carter." She tilted her gaze to meet his. Her gray-blue eyes squinted against the fall of rain as she focused in on him. "My daughter?"

Jake loosened his grip, expecting her to recoil now that she was getting a close-up look at the violence of his face. Instead, her fingers curled into his wet T-shirt, grabbing some of the skin underneath. The unfamiliar burst of heat that raced to the muscles she clung to reminded him just how long it had been since he'd had a woman in any way, shape or form. All of a sudden, he wanted this one. Badly.

She was wrong not to be afraid of him.

"Let's go," he said roughly, squashing those urges and pulling her into step beside him. Jake released her only long enough to grab the baseball bat. Even though her attacker was long gone, there was no sense in giving anyone the opportunity to be armed out here except for him.

He helped her around the van, noting that her balance grew stronger with each step, even though she was still favoring that right leg. She lost her footing once on the slick pavement and her hand flew to the middle of his chest again. Jake tried to concentrate on the accidental pinch of chest hair and not on the needy tugs on his skin that awakened something primal and male deeper inside him. He easily took her weight against his side until her wet tennis shoes found traction again.

"Emma?" She eased her death grip on his soggy T-shirt and kept moving forward, despite a hissing catch of breath.

The woman was a slender rail of shapeless raincoat and stubbornness, although the top of her flattened wet hair reached his chin. His blood boiled to think how much damage that jackass with the baseball bat might have done to her. "How bad are you hurt?" he asked, scanning back and forth as they crossed the empty parking lot for any signs of Mr. Amateur or his accomplice coming back for round three. "He didn't, um…?"

"I'll live. And no, he didn't rape me. He… You stopped him." So nothing major, although he was guessing a broken leg wouldn't have slowed her march toward the abandoned car. The crying grew louder as they approached the blue sedan. Jake had to lengthen his stride to keep up with her quickening steps. "Emma? Mommy's here."

Another flash of lightning gave Jake a better view of the car. Both of the driver's side doors were standing open and the high-pitched sobs were coming from the backseat. Robin was steady enough to break into a limping run. "Oh, my God. Emma!"

Jake let her rush ahead, sparing a few moments to make sure the lot and street and sidewalks were empty before he caught up to her. When he looked over her shoulder, he didn't like what he saw. The car seat was sitting at a wonky angle in the car and the seat belt anchoring it into place had been cut, sawed through with something sharp. Like that amateur's knife. A piece of pink material lay in a puddle on the ground outside the door. What the hell?

If the kid hadn't been bawling her lungs out, Jake would

have suspected the baby might be missing or had met an uglier fate than her mother. "Hold on." He grabbed Robin's arm before she could pick up the kid. "See if you can get her out without messing with things. This seat has been tampered with. The cops will want to see it."

"The cops... Right. I need to call 911." Through a miraculous bit of dexterity that Jake doubted his thick fingers could emulate, Robin unhooked the baby from the car seat and lifted her into her arms. "Shh, sweetie. Oh, you're all wet. Shh. You're okay now. Mommy didn't mean to leave you. I'm back. I'm here."

"The kid's not hurt, is she?"

"I don't think so. She's just unhappy." Robin tugged the soggy blanket up over the baby's head and rocked her on her shoulder, despite the pain that tightened her face. But the kid kept wailing. Did little kids that age know to be afraid? Had she been startled by the half-assed attempt to remove the car seat? Did she just not like the rain? "I wonder how long she was by herself. How long was I out? What kind of mother am I?"

The right kind, he was guessing. She'd tuned in to the baby's wailing before he had. "It's only been a few minutes since I showed up."

The blanket slipped off the infant's head, revealing wisps of brown hair and blue eyes, just like her mama's. Tears spilled over her chubby pink cheeks. Great. He'd been lusting after some baby's mother. Jake glanced at the hand rubbing the baby's back. No wedding ring. Didn't mean there wasn't a man in the picture.

Hell. What was he doing, thinking he was attracted to Robin Carter, anyway? Jake rolled the baseball bat in his grip down at his side. He didn't need the complication of a woman in his messed-up life. And he sure as hell didn't need a baby. Still, he had to admire the lungs on the kid.

Seemed about as headstrong as her mother. "Is she okay? Can she hurt herself crying like that?"

"No. Eventually, she'll cry herself back to sleep. But it breaks your heart to listen to it, doesn't it?" Robin started pacing back and forth, trying to quiet the baby without success. From what little he knew about kids, mostly from the son of a former coworker who sometimes came to the bar to visit her uncle—the bar's owner—Jake thought they picked up on the mood of the people around them. And right now, Mama here was in desperate panic mode. "Mommy was so scared, sweetie. Are you all right? The man didn't hurt you, did he? I'm not leaving you again. It's going to be okay. Mommy loves you." If anything, the kid wailed louder. "I can't seem to..." When Robin turned her pleading eyes to him, Jake realized just how tiny that baby was. Only a few months old. It didn't even look big enough to crawl yet. "Will you stay with us until the police come, Mr. Lonergan?"

Not one damsel in distress, but two. He was toast. "Yeah. I'll stay."

"Thank you." She extended her hand, expecting the civility of formal gratitude. Instead of shaking hands, though, she grabbed his wrist and bent his arm across his stomach. And then she was pushing the baby into his chest. "Do you mind? Make sure you support her neck."

"Mind what...? Oh, whoa. Hey..."

"Keep her face covered. I don't want her to get any wetter than she already is."

With careful, slow-motion control, she shrugged out of her backpack while Jake stood there in shock, afraid to move. And his nightmares were the only thing that ever scared him. "Lady, I don't think you want to—"

"Here's a dry blanket. Relatively dry, anyway." Robin draped the square of cotton flannel, dotted with pink animals, over his arm and the infant, tucking the ends securely around her. She leaned forward and pressed a kiss to her daughter's pink cheek before draping the last corner over the baby's face. "Got her?"

Did he have a choice?

"I need to call the police." Robin pulled her cell phone out of the same bag and hooked the flowered backpack over her uninjured arm. "Do you think it's okay if we go back inside the shop? I want to get her out of the rain."

She wanted him to move with the baby? The little thing stretched out, nestled her butt in his palm and turned her face into his chest as if she was settling in for the night. Hell, the thing was so tiny, he barely felt the weight of her lying across his arm. What if he stumbled? Or squeezed his big hand too hard? He was armed and dangerous, for Pete's sake. "Lady—"

"Robin." She'd already punched in the number and lifted the phone to her ear. "Call me Robin. And this is Emma." She touched the infant again and nodded toward the green-and-white awning with the Robin's Nest Floral Shop logo painted on it. "I must have wrenched my shoulder. I'd feel better if you carried her. Come on."

Okay. Fine. If Robin was hurt, he could carry the baby. Carefully watching the infant in his left arm, Jake tucked the bat beneath his right elbow and nudged Robin into step ahead of him. "Let's get you both inside."

In just a couple of minutes, all the lights were blazing inside Robin's shop and office, and Jake was more uncomfortable than before, if possible. He'd set the bat behind her office door and was pacing back and forth, from door to barred alley window, waiting for Robin to finish her conversation with the KCPD dispatcher and rescue the baby from him. Emma Carter was just so small and fragile, and he was so big and rough around the edges. He didn't think it was a far-fetched possibility that he might accidentally snap the soft little thing in two.

Subduing a creep beating up a woman in a back alley, he could handle. But holding a tiny baby? Making civil conversation? Worrying about the stiff way Robin Carter was carrying herself? Trying not to peek while she tucked in her torn blouse and refastened her belt and jeans? Not his best thing.

Making the decision to trust him had sprung from the necessity of the situation. But the unfamiliar expectations that trust engendered made him a little nervous. As soon as she was done making her report, Jake intended to have her lock the door behind him and leave.

"Hey. You've got the touch." Robin ended the call and came over to stroke Emma's cheek. "I guess she's decided she's not afraid of you, either."

It wasn't until that moment that Jake realized the kid had stopped crying. He held his breath, afraid to move in case he'd done something wrong. "Is she okay?"

"She's asleep. Haven't you been around a baby before?"

"I don't know."

"You don't know?"

Her gaze flashed up to his and Jake looked away. Normally, he didn't slip like that. But no way was he going to share the blank page of his life.

Apparently, Robin was okay with his lack of an explanation. Or just more concerned about her daughter. She touched the baby's cheek again and the little thing buzzed a tiny sigh through her pink lips. "I tried everything to get her to sleep tonight. She must feel your warmth and strength. Emma feels safe when you hold her."

This time, Robin bobbed her head, her gaze chasing his, insisting his eyes lock on to hers. Once they did, he couldn't look away from their gray-blue beauty and what just might be a hint of longing there. Like she thought it might be a good idea if he held *her,* too.

The last thing Jake needed was a distraction like that. He'd already spent too much time with the Carter girls. The smell of baby powder and flowers filled his nose. The baby's implicit trust in him was already short-circuiting the perimeter he liked to keep between him and other people. He didn't need Robin Carter's more womanly scent clinging to him, too, lingering on his skin and clothes when he got back to his apartment, reminding him of everything that was missing from his life.

A woman and a child were things normal men had. Men cursed as he was couldn't afford the indulgence.

Best to clear all those warm fuzzies out of his head right now. He handed Emma back to Robin and purposely retreated beyond arm's length. "She's just exhausted because it's so late."

"When she's too tired, she usually fusses all the more. I think she likes you."

"I hope her taste in men improves as she gets older."

"Don't." Robin's eyes snapped back to his.

"Don't what?" He could see her bottom lip quivering despite the reprimand in her eyes. She was rethinking her decision about seeking help from such a villainous-looking stranger.

But she pressed those expressive lips together and pushed aside whatever doubt she was feeling. "I don't know who you are, Mr. Lonergan. But I know who you are tonight. And I won't have you trash-talking the man who saved me and my daughter."

Huh? She was lecturing him? Most people scared off a lot easier than this woman did. A harsh glance or gruff word usually nipped any overtures of friendship in the bud. She was a stubborn one. Or crazy.

He watched how gently Robin carried the sleeping infant to the white bassinet in the corner and unsnapped the fuzzy yellow sleeper she was wearing. She undressed the baby, diapered her, put on a clean sleeping outfit and cap without the kid making another peep. "I don't see any marks on her. She may just have been in the way of whatever that man wanted."

"Thugs with knives and baseball bats don't steal car seats."

"He had a knife, too?" She gave him a sharp glance, then winced at the sudden movement.

"He pulled it on me. Used it to slice through that seat belt, too, I'm guessing. You're lucky he didn't cut you."

The color in her cheeks was fading again. "So why hurt Emma if he wanted to rape me?"

"I'm guessing he just wanted her out of the way. She'd be dead if that was what he wanted."

Robin's weary sigh made him regret the harsh honesty. She covered Emma with the flannel blanket before looking at him. "You're not much for giving a girl hope, are you?"

Nah. He wasn't much of one for hope of any kind.

Better stick to the tough words and keeping his distance to remind himself that spending these few minutes with Robin and Emma Carter was a one-time thing. He could save her from being raped or worse. But he couldn't do the whole you're-my-hero domestic bliss thing. "So what were you two doing out so late in this part of town?"

Robin opened a cabinet behind her desk and pulled out a thin baby towel that she tossed across the room to him. Apparently, he'd finally made his desire to keep some distance between them clear. He dried his face and arms while she pulled out a second towel to dab at her own pale skin. "I own this shop. Emma usually doesn't fall asleep for the night until around eleven or twelve. I thought I'd take advantage of her schedule and catch up on some work."

"Well, don't do it again."

"No. I won't." She towel-dried her hair, scrunching it into sable-colored waves that framed her face. "I shouldn't have let work take over like that. I was worried something was wrong and I wanted to fix…" She stopped that excuse on a purposeful sigh. "I know better. With the Rose Red Rapist still around… Do you think that was him?"

Jake shrugged. Even amongst criminals there was a hierarchy of what was acceptable and what was not. A lowlife who preyed on a woman with a small baby in tow was pretty low on the list—at least in Jake's book.

Maybe she hadn't gotten the distance message, after all. She circled the desk and plucked the damp towel from his hands. "Did you get a look at his face? All I saw was the mask…and the baseball bat. When he dragged me behind the van, I thought…" She hugged the wadded-up towels to her chest and that full bottom lip quivered again. Jake's human impulse was to reach out and offer some kind of comfort. But his survival instincts curled his fingers into a fist down at his side, instead. "All I could think of was that I had to stay alive for Emma's sake."

"Yeah." He wasn't real comfortable making small talk and keeping her company until the police arrived on the scene—even though he knew several of the officers and detectives in this precinct because they frequented the Shamrock Bar where he worked most nights. He was even less comfortable with the unfamiliar desire to pull those slender shoulders against his chest and shield her from the fear that lingered in her eyes.

No connections. No commitments. No caring.

Those were the three Cs he'd lived by for the past two years. They were the only way he could guarantee that the nightmares from his forgotten life couldn't come back and destroy anyone else before he had the chance to remember the truth—good or bad—and to deal with it.

"Mr. Lonergan?" He realized she was still waiting for him to answer her question. "Did you see him?"

"I didn't see his face." She carried the towels to a hamper beside the bassinet and dropped them inside. "But he was short for a man—not much taller than you. And he could run like the devil."

"Would you have tried to capture him if you weren't worried about me?"

Jake considered the honest answer. True, he couldn't have run the guy down. But he could have pulled the gun from his ankle holster and shot him—probably hit his mark, too. Even in the dark. In the rain. Although he hadn't shot a man in the two years he *could* remember, Jake had the strongest feeling that he was able to make a shot like that. How else could a man handle a knife the way he could, and know so much about weaponry and choke holds and throwing a punch?

But there was honest, and then there was too much honesty. He suspected that informing Robin Carter he carried both a gun and a hunting knife, and that he possessed the skills to use them better than most, wouldn't give her the reassurance she was looking for right now. He shook his head. "One good deed for the night's all I got in me."

"I asked you not to say things like that."

"Look, lady—"

"Robin," she corrected him. "I also asked you to call me Robin."

He blew out a long sigh, conceding to her will—for the few moments longer he intended to be a part of her life. "Robin. You don't really know me. You shouldn't automatically trust me."

"I trusted you because I had to. You haven't disappointed me yet."

Oh, hell. That sounded like some sort of relationship had been forged between them.

Jake was relieved as much as he was on edge when he heard the sirens in the distance outside. He nodded toward the back door where they'd come in. "You stay here with the kid. I'll wait outside and show the police in."

It was one thing to serve a cop a drink. It was something else to stand there and answer his questions, maybe come under scrutiny himself for wandering the streets so late at night. And being armed the way he was bound to raise a few suspicions.

Jake surmised the distance and direction of the approaching flashing lights. He paused for one shameless moment to admire the apple-shaped curve of Robin Carter's backside, emphasized by the clinging hug of her wet jeans, as she bent over the bassinet, tending to her sleeping baby again.

The cops were close enough. She'd be safe.

"Thank you again, Mr. Lonergan. By the way, you never told me your first name…"

He never heard the end of her sentence. By the time she straightened from the bassinet, he was gone.

Chapter Three

"You take care of whatever you need to and don't worry about Emma." Hope Lockhart pulled her toffee-blond hair from beneath Emma's head where it nestled on her ample bosom and shook the loose, sleep-rumpled curls down her back. "I'll take her across the street and get the spare room ready for you two. It'll be a lot quieter in my apartment and she can sleep. You know I like hanging out with sweetie-pie here."

Robin followed her friend into the hallway outside her office and pulled the blanket up over her sleeping daughter's head. "I'm so glad you came over, Hope. Thank you."

"Not a problem. When I heard the sirens and saw all the lights… You know what I thought." Hope's fearful expression echoed what every woman thought whenever KCPD, reporters and an ambulance gathered in this part of Kansas City—the Rose Red Rapist had claimed another victim.

Robin adjusted the ice pack over her bruised shoulder and gave her friend a hug. "I'm okay. At least, I will be once all the craziness calms down."

When she pulled away, Hope's deep gray eyes had narrowed into a frown behind the glasses she wore. She was looking beyond Robin's shoulder to the three KCPD investigators inside her office. "Can't you tell these people to go away and leave you alone, at least until daylight? It's not fair that the victim has to deal with all this after being attacked. I don't think I could handle so many people poking into my life, wanting something from me."

Robin summoned a smile as she pulled together the gaping collar of the trench coat Hope had thrown on over her nightgown before running downstairs from her apartment above the Fairy Tale Bridal Shop she owned across the street. Her shy friend was stronger than she gave herself credit for. "Who came charging over here in the middle of the night when she thought Emma or I might be hurt?"

"I didn't stop to think about it—I just did it. And you *are* hurt." Hope tucked a damp, frizzing tendril behind her ear. "But talking to those detectives in your office without stumbling over my words and sounding like an idiot? Trust me, I'd rather babysit."

"Well, I'm grateful." Robin leaned in and pressed a goodbye kiss to Emma's soft, warm cheek. She pulled back with a stern, sisterly warning for her friend. "Make sure one of the officers walks you across the street. Even that short distance isn't safe anymore."

"I will. I saw Maggie Wheeler outside, blocking off the parking lot with crime scene tape. She's a client of mine. I'm planning her wedding to that Marine, remember? I ordered her flowers through you—"

"Detective Montgomery?" The back door slammed shut and a man's deep voice called out, interrupting Hope's soft gasp. The pungent smell of wet dog tickled Robin's nose a split second before Hope hugged Emma tightly to her chest and retreated a step.

"Hope? What is it?" Robin turned at her friend's stricken expression to see a K-9 officer with his brown-and-tan German shepherd partner striding down the hallway. The dog paused when his handler did, and shook himself from nose to tail. The cop pulled off his black KCPD ball cap and knocked the excess water against his pant leg, leaving a similar spray of water droplets on the concrete floor.

"Detective Montgomery?" The officer rapped sharply on the frame of the door to Robin's office. His square jaw warmed with a shade of pink when he realized the two women were staring at him. "Sorry, ma'am. If you point me to a mop, I can clean up after Hans and me."

Robin suspected the blush on those rugged features meant the apology was sincere. "That's okay. I deal with plenty of water around all these flowers. That's why the floor is sealed and the walls have moisture-resistant wallpaper. I'll wait until everyone's done before I tackle the footprints and rain we've all tracked in."

"Pike?" Spencer Montgomery, the red-haired detective who seemed to be running this whole show, looked up from the notepad where he'd been jotting information and joined them at the doorway. He tucked the notepad and pen inside the pocket of his suit jacket. "Did you two find anything?"

"Rain's washed away any scent we can track." The nameplate on the officer's uniform identified him as E. Taylor. Pike must be a nickname. "Looks like there was a scuffle in the alley, though—away from the loading dock where Ms. Carter said she ended up. The perp could have escaped through there easily enough. As for the man you claim rescued you—"

"He did."

"—I've got no clue where he disappeared to. There's no car, no footprints, no sign of him anywhere."

Spencer Montgomery nodded. "His sudden departure might mean he has reason to avoid talking to the police."

The need to defend the man who'd saved her life

charged Robin's weary body with renewed energy. "And it might mean he had to get to work at an early morning job. Or go home to his family."

As soon as she said the words, Robin wondered if there was any truth to them. There was something about Mr. No-Name Lonergan—his reluctance to hold Emma, his gruff demeanor and brute strength, that odd comment he'd made about not knowing if there were any children in his life—that made Robin think he was a man without any familial connections to civilize him. What kind of man roamed a downtown neighborhood in the middle of the night during a storm without benefit of umbrella, raincoat or even a cap? Where had he come from? Why had he disappeared? Where had he learned that chokehold thing he'd done to her attacker? He'd never given her his first name, and she'd been too out of it to even think to ask. What if Lonergan *was* a criminal? He certainly looked the part of a TV or movie villain with that scarred face and misshapen nose that indicated he'd seen more than one fight in his lifetime.

But something about the sense of isolation that had fit him as tightly as the T-shirt he'd worn tugged at her compassion. She didn't suppose he owed her anything, not even the courtesy of a proper goodbye. But she owed him everything. Bad guy or not, he'd been her hero. Robin swore to herself, not for the first time that night, that she would track down her mysterious savior and thank him properly for being there when she and Emma had needed him.

"Maybe." The detective seemed to consider her reasoning and then dismissed any option but his own. Lonergan was still a person of interest, if not a viable suspect, on his list. Spencer Montgomery glanced up at the K-9 officer and gave his orders. "Keep an eye on things until the CSI's are done processing the scene. And keep those damn reporters out of everyone's way. We'll debrief later this morning."

"Yes, sir." After he'd been dismissed, and the lead detective had returned to his conversation with his partner in her office, the brawny K-9 officer looked down at Hope, still frozen in place beside Robin, and winked. "Hans won't hurt you, ma'am. Not unless I tell him to." The officer's teasing grin vanished when Hope's eyes widened like circles rippling across a lake. He quickly raised a gloved hand. "But I would never give him that order. I just meant he only does what I tell him to. Ma'am?"

"Hope?" Robin reached for her friend. "He was teasing you."

"I know." But the tight press of her lips and ashy skin indicated that what she knew and what she believed weren't the same thing. "He's a cop. He's a good guy."

"Maybe Officer Taylor could walk you and Emma home," Robin suggested.

"No!" Her friend's answer was too fast and too succinct to be polite and her cheeks instantly flooded with embarrassment.

"I don't mind," the big man offered. "Security is what Hans and I do best."

"No." Hope's gaze darted up to meet Pike Taylor's, but then settled, almost deliberately, at the middle of his chest. "I mean, no, thank you. Officer Wheeler's outside. She's a friend. I'll ask her."

Robin's concern shifted from defending Lonergan to the situation at hand. The Hope she knew was a gentle, patient soul—not this skittish woman who was visibly shaking in her soggy slippers.

"Hope?" She put a hand beneath Emma before touching her friend's shoulder.

Hope snapped her gaze to Robin. "I've got her," Hope reassured her, hugging the infant in her arms. And though she sounded more like the friend Robin relied on, Hope's gaze was darting from the officer's chest down to the dog, where he lay on the floor, panting, while his tongue lolled out of the side of his long black muzzle. The shepherd looked completely relaxed and disinterested in the people coming and going around him. Her friend, however, seemed ready to bolt. "I'll go find Maggie Wheeler. You still have the spare key I gave you?"

"Yes. I'll let myself in."

Hope forced a smile and flattened her back against the wall to scoot around the police officer and his dog. "Emma and I will be at home when you're done. Good luck."

She'd disappeared through the heavy steel door to the parking lot before Officer Taylor spoke. "Did I do something wrong? Is she okay?"

There was shy and tongue-tied, and then there was freaking out. Robin shrugged her confusion, then winced at the pain radiating through her shoulder. "I honestly don't know. I've never seen her act like that before."

"Sorry I scared her. I would never sic Hans on her."

Robin nodded, adding her friend's behavior to the list of things that perplexed her tonight. "I know."

"Well, we'd best be getting back to work. Ma'am." Officer Taylor put his cap back on and tipped the bill to her before tugging on the dog's collar and giving a command in German that prompted the dog to its feet and into step beside him.

Left alone for a few quiet moments, away from the chaos that had descended on her shop and the parking lot outside, Robin inhaled a steadying breath. Part of her wanted to go after Hope to find out what had upset her so, and part of her wanted to curl up in bed with Emma so they could get some sleep and recapture the serenity of their life before the man with the baseball bat.

But Robin knew she wouldn't be much help to her friend, nor would there be any real relaxing, until she finished her interview with the police and got her life back to its normal routine. If *normal* was even possible.

While she considered herself infinitely practical, and was used to dealing with the problems in her life on her own, something in Robin's world had shifted tonight. Her confidence had been rattled and, for the first time, she wondered if she'd been selfish to bring Emma into her life. She'd wanted a family to fill her big house and empty heart so badly that she'd jumped at the chance to adopt Emma when her birth mother had terminated her parental rights. But maybe she had no business being a single mom. Tonight she'd been terrified—not just for herself, but for Emma. She'd been helpless to defend herself or her daughter.

And then Lonergan showed up out of nowhere. Despite his ghostlike appearance, he was solid and real. She'd leaned on him when she'd been too weak to stand and too frightened to think, and he hadn't budged an inch. Robin didn't doubt that he could kill a man with those big hands of his—he'd tossed that creep aside like a bag of trash. Yet he'd cradled Emma as though she was the most fragile treasure in the world.

He'd been growly and gruff and overwhelming, and had no interest in accepting the proper thanks he deserved. Still, Lonergan's sudden disappearance left a void in her world. Any real sense of security was gone. She was usually such a good judge of people. Hadn't she sensed some sort of interest in his icy gaze? Even if it wasn't sexual, she was certain that there'd been a connection between them.

But gone was gone. She had no idea why one man would come after her, and another would run away.

"Ms. Carter?" Spencer Montgomery was at the doorway again, waiting for her to come in to finish answering his questions. "Is the baby settled?"

With a nod that was more a surrender to the inevitable than an answer to his question, Robin followed him back into her office.

"CSI Hermann needs to process you." Detective Montgomery introduced the petite brunette woman wearing a blue CSI vest. "Is it all right if she does that while we finish our interview?"

"Of course." Since shooing them out and holing up with her daughter for a couple of hours wasn't an option, Robin offered them a cooperative smile, instead. "Did you find that woman I saw earlier? Did she get home safely?"

Detective Montgomery shook his head. "Your description was pretty vague, but there have been no other assaults reported. I've got street patrols keeping an eye out for her, just in case, but they haven't spotted anyone else."

"It looks as though the attack tonight was all about you." *Oh, goody.* Spencer Montgomery's partner, Nick Fensom, pulled out the chair behind her desk and invited her to sit. He was shorter than his partner, dark-haired and stocky. Even his jeans and leather jacket were a contrast to his suit-and-tie associate. "You were about to tell us why you stayed late after work tonight?"

Right. That mess. Numbers that wouldn't balance seemed insignificant compared to her daughter being thrust into danger and nearly dying herself.

"I've been on maternity leave for a couple of months," she explained, squeezing her fingers between her knees in her lap to stop their sudden trembling. "When I came back to work this week, I discovered there were some discrepancies in my books. Money missing. On paper, anyway. Since Emma wasn't sleeping, I thought I could use the time to try and figure out where the problem is."

Detective Fensom pointed to the wrinkled files and printouts that had been in the rain-soaked diaper bag with Emma's things. Now the damp papers were in sealed bags and labeled as evidence on her desk. "Did you find the problem?"

"No. I was going to take them home and study them there. I'd already disrupted my daughter's routine more than I should."

"Do you think someone's stealing money from you?" he asked.

"The people who work for me are also my friends." Did she have to defend everyone who was on her side tonight?

The detective shrugged. "Sometimes, even friends can run into trouble and resort to doing something desperate."

"None of my friends attacked me." Robin tilted her chin up as the conversation went off on a whole new tangent about how long she'd known her employees, and how well did she trust them? She promised a list of names and addresses, as well.

Holding an ice pack over the deep bruise on her collarbone, Robin turned her head while Annie Hermann snapped a photo of Robin's hand and then proceeded to scrape beneath her fingernails, collecting whatever she'd scratched off her attacker into a small manila envelope. "Looks like you got some trace off your attacker," the criminologist speculated. "If we're lucky, there'll be enough here to get DNA."

Nick Fensom shook his head. "Since when have we ever been lucky with this guy?" The CSI flashed him a chastising look and the detective quickly apologized to Robin.

"Other than you turning this attack into an *attempted* rape, Ms. Carter, and not getting hurt any worse than you did."

The EMT had said she was lucky, too. She might have a broken back and be paralyzed or dead if it hadn't been for the diaper bag cushioning the most critical blows. As for the rape? She was still unsure why he'd opted for clubbing her in the head rather than pulling her pants down the rest of the way and completing the awful deed.

But luck had nothing to do with her surviving tonight. A mysterious man had stepped out of the shadows and saved her.

"Are you sure you didn't see him?" Robin asked, turning the conversation away from accounting, serial rapists and possible motives. "He's hard to miss. I can describe him for you."

"Your attacker?"

"No. The man who rescued us." She shifted uncomfortably in her chair as CSI Hermann processed the other hand. Robin owed him a lot more than a thank-you. "He had a broken nose."

Spencer Montgomery pulled out his notebook again. "He got hurt?"

Robin shook her head, pointing out the details as if the marks were on her own skin. "They were old injuries. His nose was crooked and had one of those bumps from where it healed wrong. And he had scars—one here—" She traced a line along her jaw to her chin. "And there was one up here, running above his ear at his temple. He wore a buzz cut and his hair was silvery white."

"He was an old guy?" Detective Fensom asked.

"Not with muscles like that. He was my age, maybe. Pale blue eyes. Very…" *Masculine.* She couldn't think of a better way to describe her rescuer. He'd been all man, with no soft edges to lessen the feral impact he'd had on her.

"He was very…?" Detective Montgomery waited for her to finish her description.

She could hardly say that her senses were still humming with feminine awareness now that the shock of the attack and fear for Emma's safety had receded. "When I was lying on the ground and first saw him, I thought he was a ghost. Or a giant. I don't know that he was unusually tall—six-two, maybe. Not as tall as your Officer Taylor." She stretched out her uninjured arm, indicating the breadth of those shoulders and chest. "But he was big. This is a guy who works out. He looked…dangerous."

"Does this ghost have a name?" Detective Montgomery paused with his pen hovering over his notepad. "I don't like it when potential witnesses flee the scene."

At least the relentlessly inquisitive detective hadn't called him a suspect. "He wasn't fleeing. I get the idea he's not a very social kind of a guy. I asked Mr. Lonergan if he saw the man who attacked me, and he couldn't tell me any more details than the description I gave you. He stopped the attack. Got us safely inside. I don't think he saw the need to stick around." The two detectives exchanged a curious look across her desk when she mentioned her rescuer's name. "What? Do you know him?"

Nick Fensom gave his partner a curt nod, and then excused himself from the conversation and exited the room. "I'll check it out."

"You *do* know him." Ignoring both pain and fatigue, Robin pushed to her feet and laid a hand on the sleeve of Spencer Montgomery's light gray suit. "I don't care if he's on your most-wanted list. Please don't pester him. I don't want to get him into trouble. He saved my life."

"It's my job to pester people. If I don't ask questions, I don't get answers. And I like answers." Pulling away without betraying his suspicions about Lonergan, he folded up his notebook and tucked it away. "Is there anything else you can tell me about the attack?"

Other than the fact there wasn't a muscle in her body that didn't feel battered and in need of a long, hot bath? Robin shook her head. "I'd like to get back to my daughter. Are we finished?"

"For now. CSI Hermann and her team need to finish processing your car before you can drive it home."

With her home nearly forty minutes away out in the Missouri countryside, and dawn ready to peek around the corner in another hour or two, that wasn't going to happen. "We'll be staying in town tonight. At my friend Hope Lockhart's apartment across the street."

The detective nodded, added that information to his notepad, and turned to the dark-haired CSI still labeling items and packing her evidence kit. "Do you need anything else, Annie?"

CSI Hermann looked up from her work and frowned an apology to Robin. "Just so you know, we removed the severed seat belt so we can take it back to the lab and compare tool marks to see what kind of blade was used."

One more thing for Robin's to-do list—get her damaged car into the shop for repairs. "I understand."

"We need to take the car seat, too, and the sleeper your daughter was wearing. We've already dusted for prints, but if the perp left any evidence behind—"

"He was wearing gloves."

With a sigh that sounded like frustration, Annie Hermann brushed the dark curls off her forehead, giving Robin a glimpse of a fresh pink scar in her hairline. "I'm familiar with that scenario. But there could be a fiber or some other kind of transfer left behind that we can use."

"I already changed her to keep her dry. Her clothes are here in the hamper." Robin turned to get them, pulling out the baby towels she and Lonergan had dried off with and reaching back inside. But the criminologist asked her to stay put. She waved her gloved—sterile—fingers in the air as she circled the desk to collect Emma's things.

Feeling that unfamiliar helplessness again, Robin hugged the damp towels to her chest and watched the woman bag and label Emma's clothes. Since she wasn't physically being allowed to do anything to reclaim control over her life tonight, Robin's brain went to work. She put together Annie Hermann's scar and frustration, and finally placed the younger woman's face from shots she'd seen on the evening news. "You're the CSI who was attacked at that murder scene on New Year's Eve."

"Yes, ma'am."

"Did you catch him?"

"We did." The younger woman's gaze bounced away, seeking out Nick Fensom as he reappeared in the doorway. Although he had a phone stuck to his ear, his blue eyes narrowed and focused on the petite brunette. She nodded at some unspoken message and turned back to Robin with a businesslike smile. "Unfortunately, the man was an accomplice, cleaning up after the Rose Red Rapist. Our serial rapist still eludes us—as does the woman who hired my attacker."

"A woman?" Stunned by her answer, Robin set the towels on the corner of her desk and laid the ice pack on top. She'd read in the *Kansas City Journal* about the task force's suspicion that the serial rapist had an accomplice who helped erase evidence of the crime after each attack. But how could any female want to help a monster like the Rose Red Rapist?

"Yes. Before my attacker died, he indicated that he'd been blackmailed into covering up the crimes by a woman." She paled as she relived what must have been a terrifying experience for her.

Nick Fensom disconnected his call and tucked the phone into his pocket as he strode across the room. He curled his fingers around Annie's and squeezed her hand. The movement was subtle, probably unnoticeable to anyone who wasn't already curious about the relationship between the two of them. "Everything okay, slugger?"

There was no doubt that the two of them cared deeply for each other because Annie Hermann's cheeks warmed with color at even that simple contact. She summoned a smile to ease his concern. "I'm okay."

Robin wasn't the only one in the room who'd noticed the trading of comforts between the stocky detective and the CSI.

"You two get back to work." Spencer Montgomery excused his coworkers from the room before stopping across the desk from Robin and handing her one of his business cards. "If you think of anything else, give me a call."

"Wait a minute, Detective. Everything I've read about your task force says that the Rose Red Rapist abducts his victims and rapes them at another location."

"That's right."

"Then why did he…rip my clothes right there in the alley? Like he was going to hurt me there?"

"Maybe you foiled the initial attack by fighting back so hard. You messed with his routine. He lost his temper." She could tell he was only speculating possible explanations.

"If that man was trying to rape me…" She breathed through that frightening possibility before voicing her real concern. "Then why endanger my daughter? Why bother cutting up my backseat? He said he didn't want the car. What *did* he want?"

"I can't answer that yet." His cool gray eyes narrowed, as though assessing whether or not she could handle his response. She must look stronger than she was feeling at the moment because he continued. "After the Rose Red Rapist attacks this past year, our task force looks into any type of assault against a woman in this neighborhood. There's an outside chance your attacker is the man we've been looking for, and something you did put him off his game. He could be copycat. He might have targeted you for some other reason. Any information we get that eliminates suspects helps us as much clues that point us to our unsub do."

"Unsub?"

"Unknown suspect. Even without the mission of this task force, I'm a cop. We don't like criminals hurting anyone here in Kansas City. Whether this attack is related to my investigation or not, I intend to look into it thoroughly."

"Good. Because I like answers, too." Answers to why her business was either missing money or keeping shoddy records in her absence. Answers to why that man had singled her out tonight—was she just a crime of opportunity because she'd stayed late? Or had she been targeted for more personal, more unsettling, reasons?

Seeming to appreciate that she was on the same page with him, the red-haired detective extended his hand across the desk. "Be safe, Ms. Carter. I'll be in touch."

Robin shook his hand. "Thank you."

He left her office and turned down the hallway toward the workroom and back exit.

Robin picked up the wadded towels and wiped the lingering moisture from the corner of her desk. She tossed the ice pack into the freezer of her mini-fridge and started to gather her things to follow Hope and Emma to the apartment across the street.

But Robin didn't get very far before the ache in her shoulder, the weight on her mind and the emptiness of her office suddenly overwhelmed her. She sank into the desk chair and hugged the towels to her chest, unsure whether she felt like cursing or crying. Her body was exhausted, her brain weary, and yet, she was too revved up to sleep. She couldn't drop her guard like that again. She had Emma's well-being to consider, not just her own. How could she make a selfish choice like working late, relying on a silly whistle to keep her safe? Only one thing had made her feel safe tonight. Only one thing had finally quieted Emma.

Lonergan. He looked more like the muscle-bound henchmen she'd seen in a dozen action-adventure movies than he did any Hollywood heartthrob.

And yet tonight, he'd been her hero.

She lifted the towels to her face and buried her nose in their cool dampness. The scent of her rescuer still lingered there, spicy and clean—dangerous, somehow. More dangerous than any threat lurking out there in the dark streets. *That* was what she needed to feel safe and in control of her world again. What she needed to keep her daughter safe. *He* was what she needed. No one could make her afraid if he was around.

Except maybe the man himself.

Ignoring a twinge of common sense that warned her she was putting her hope in someone she didn't completely understand, Robin dropped the towels and dashed into the hallway to catch up with Spencer Montgomery.

"Detective?" Montgomery turned as he shrugged into a dark blue KCPD raincoat at the shop's back door. "If you find Mr. Lonergan, would you let me know? I'd like to thank him."

The detective offered her a curt nod before following his partner and the CSI out the back door.

Chapter Four

Forty minutes later, Robin shut off the lights in the empty shop and turned, breathing in the familiar scents of freesia, gardenias and chemical preservatives. Guided by the lights inside the refrigerated display case opposite the front counter, she opened a glass door and pulled out a lavender gladiolus that was sagging over the edge of its pot.

She looked at the broken stem in her hand, recognizing the tidying up for the stall tactic it was. With a groan of disgust at her seeming inability to function with any sense of urgency, she tossed the wilted flower into the trash and headed to her office. "Get out of here, Robin," she chided herself.

There was no reason for her to be afraid to leave. KCPD felt confident enough in the security of her building that they had all gone. There was no more ambulance in the parking lot, no cadre of reporters waiting on the sidewalk for a glimpse of the Rose Red Rapist's latest alleged "victim," no reason to be fearful inside the business where she'd spent so many happy, hardworking, successful hours of her life.

She crossed the lobby to check the front door again, even though it had never been unlocked since she'd closed it at nine. Bolted tight. Alarm sensors on.

She could relax her guard and leave now, right?

Only, there wasn't a brain cell in her head or a bruised muscle on her body that seemed to be relaxing.

The rain outside was still coming down in buckets, although the thunder and lightning had finally eased their fury. An eerie sense of déjà vu washed over her. Not five hours ago, she'd stood in the same place, thinking of how the rain nourished her flowers and grass. Her biggest concerns had been a few lousy numbers and a daughter who wouldn't sleep. She'd felt more confident—more naive, perhaps—the last time she'd stared out this window. Five hours ago, she'd mistakenly thought that a purposeful walk and a steel whistle would keep her and Emma safe.

Now she was more aware. More alert. More suspicious of the dangers that lay in wait for them out there in the night.

Raising her chin against the wary uncertainty she wasn't used to feeling, Robin's gaze tilted up to the row of windows over the Fairy Tale Bridal shop. Hope had turned a light on in the guest bedroom, no doubt as a courtesy for her late arrival. Robin's mouth eased into a smile. She wasn't alone. She didn't have far to go to find warmth and welcome and a chance to regain the emotional equilibrium tonight's attack had stolen from her.

The smile lingered on her lips as she let her gaze follow the line of windows to the end of the redbrick building. She nodded, telling herself she was reassured by the security camera and lights installed at the corner of Hope's shop. Detective Montgomery had already requested any footage that might have recorded Robin's attack. She could do this. She could be independent again. Like any other challenge she'd faced in her life, she'd refuse to let the fear defeat her.

Almost hyperaware of her surroundings now, on guard against any threat that might approach her or Emma again,

Robin dropped her gaze down the sidewalk, past the row of cars parked there for the night, visually scoping out the path she'd take across the street. She followed the wooden, ivy-twined fence that framed the parking lot beside Hope's shop. Gaining confidence with every moment of this silent pep talk, she looked into the emptiness of the alley beyond that fence and…her heart stopped.

"Lonergan."

She breathed his name. Leaning closer to the window, she peered through the rain, fogging up the glass for a moment as she identified the ghost lurking in the shadows. Arms folded across that massive chest, leaning against the bricks at the edge of the alley across the street. Black T-shirt, broad shoulders, silver hair.

Icy blue eyes meeting hers.

"Lonergan!" she shouted, pulling away from the window. Recognition jump-started her focus out of that anxious lethargy. Purpose energized her steps.

Robin ran through the swinging doors into the hallway and dashed into her office where she grabbed her raincoat and purse. She stuffed Hope's spare keys into the pocket of her jeans and ran through the workrooms. She never questioned the anticipation coursing through her, never wondered what propelled her out that thick steel door.

He'd stayed. He'd come back. He was still watching over her, protecting her.

She had to see him, had to thank him, had to find out his damned first name.

The splash of cold rain on her skin startled her from the blindly eager rush. She paused beneath the edge of the awning to pull on her coat and blink the moisture from her lashes. By the time she'd cleared her vision, he was gone.

"Son of a…" Slightly breathless and unsure whether she felt disappointment or anger, she clutched her slicker together at the neck and trained her gaze onto the alley where she'd seen him. She moved closer to the street, looked up to the stoplight on the corner and deliberately scanned her way down the block, past every recessed entryway and parked car where he might hide. "Why are you doing this to me?"

Her gaze stopped at a dark green sedan, parked next to the entrance to Fairy Tale Bridal. Her breath stopped, too. It filled up her chest and squeezed out any false sense of security she'd felt at seeing Lonergan again.

There was a man inside the car, dressed in dark clothes. But there was no startling thatch of silver-white hair, no battered face—no face at all that she could see—only shadows.

Feeling his eyes on her as surely as she'd felt Lonergan's, Robin instinctively backed away. She'd go back into the shop. Call 911. Demand to speak to Spencer Montgomery and tell him there was someone outside the shop again. The same man who'd attacked her? Someone else?

Since she couldn't see his face, for all she knew, the man could be sleeping and was no threat at all. Still, that possibility of danger, that hypercharged suspicion of the unknown, prompted her retreat. Keeping her eyes on the car, she backed up beneath the awning until her fingers brushed against the reassuring hardness of hard, cold steel.

"Ma'am?"

Robin screamed. A dog barked and she screamed again as she spun toward the uniformed officer and his German shepherd. She clutched her hand to the quick rise and fall of her chest, unable to summon anything resembling relief. "Officer Taylor. You startled me."

"Sorry." He held up a gloved hand in apologetic surrender and backed away a step. "I don't make a habit out of scaring people, I swear. Detective Montgomery asked for a volunteer to patrol the neighborhood and I…I just…" His blond eyebrows arched into a frown as he fumbled for the words he wanted to say. "I felt so bad about your friend earlier, Hans and I wanted to hang around to make sure you got to where you're going."

"I'm only going across the street." When she pointed toward Hope's apartment, and Pike Taylor's attention shifted to the bridal shop, the engine of the car that had alarmed her turned over and roared to life. Pike's shoulders straightened, taking note of the green car pulling out and disappearing over the rise of the intersection at the top of the street.

Had the uniformed officer scared off the driver? Or was the sudden departure a mere coincidence?

Pike Taylor wasn't taking any chances. "Across town or across the street, we'd be happy to walk you, ma'am." Clearly, his vow to serve and protect was no joke to him. "I wanted to do the same for Miss Lockhart, but she wouldn't… I mean, she was more comfortable with Officer Wheeler. Maggie's a good cop, don't get me wrong, but I'm not a horrible… I'm rambling, aren't I?"

Her terror eased into something approaching motherly concern at his struggle to express himself. Robin inhaled a deep breath that seemed to calm them both. "I'd be relieved to have you walk me over to Hope's apartment."

"Okay." With a brusque command to Hans, the three of them crossed the parking lot. Robin noticed how Pike Taylor's gaze scanned up and down the street with every step, just as Lonergan's had when he'd taken her and Emma inside the shop.

Robin, too, searched the lights and shadows as they stepped off the curb. "Did you see him?"

"The guy in the green sedan?"

"No, the…" Lonergan was gone. Again. He was a mystery who fascinated as much as he frustrated her. But the message was clear. For whatever reason, he wanted nothing more to do with her. He'd said he had only one good deed in him, and she'd already taxed his quota for the night.

She tried to block out her curiosity about her rescuer and concentrate on the young man beside her. "So staying late is Hans's idea, too?"

Pike Taylor grinned. "The two of us think a lot alike."

Robin smiled at the idea of a man and his dog thinking as one. "My friend Hope bought the bottom two floors of this building from the same man who sold me my space across the street. She's converted the entire level above her bridal shop into storage and a generous-size apartment."

"I remember her, from interviews and security sweeps early in our task force investigation. She usually wears her hair all up in a bun so I didn't recognize her tonight. I thought she was older." He followed Robin through the parking lot gate to the building's side entrance. "She's not."

Robin was beginning to wonder if Pike's interest in Hope had to do with something other than guilt. "She's younger than me," Robin assured him. They reached the brick archway framing the door and she pulled out the keys to unlock both the outer entrance and the inside door that led upstairs to the private apartment. "Thanks for the company." She smiled up to the man holding the glass door for her and then looked down to her other escort. "Is he friendly?"

"Unless I tell him not to be."

"May I?" Pike nodded at her request to pet the sleekly muscular dog. Feeling the closest thing to normalcy that she had all night, she scratched around the shepherd's wet ears. When he pressed his head up against her palm in silent approval, she petted him again. "Thank you, too, Hans. Now you tell this big guy to get you a treat and a warm, dry place to sleep for what's left of tonight."

"I will." Pike tipped the bill of his KCPD cap and twisted his mouth with a wry smile. "And, please, give my apologies to Miss Lockhart. I'm really not that scary of a guy."

Tilting her face into the rain to assess his height and the equally brawny dog at his side, Robin begged to differ. But there was such a boyish earnestness in his blue eyes, she didn't have the heart to argue. "I'll tell her. And thanks."

Such a simple word—*thanks.* Such a relief to get to express gratitude where it was due.

"You're welcome, ma'am. Good night."

"Good night." Robin bolted the door behind her and watched as Pike and Hans jogged back across the street. She turned to unlock the door that led to the upstairs apartment when she heard a sharp rap on the glass behind her.

Wishing her startle mechanism had fritzed out for the night so she'd stop jumping at every little noise or movement, Robin pressed a hand to her racing heart and turned—fearing her attacker had returned, hoping Pike Taylor had forgotten something.

She didn't expect to see a ghost.

"Lonergan," she whispered, quickly unlocking the outer door and pushing it open. "I thought I saw you. You came back."

He squinted against the rain pelting his face. "Are you and the kid okay?"

"Yes, I..." She invited him to step into the vestibule, but wasn't surprised when he chose to remain out in the elements. Somehow, the unforgiving downpour that soaked his hair and plastered his shirt to every intimidating cord of muscle fit his wild, dangerous looks. Fine. He had an

aversion to civility? Then she'd enter his domain. Letting
the door close behind her, she joined him out in the parking lot. Her hood fell back and the rain chilled her skin
even as her temper brewed. "What kind of game are you
playing? The police wanted to talk to you. What's with
the magician's act of showing up and disappearing without a word?"

"I wanted to make sure you got from point A to point
B without another incident. Glad Officer Taylor there had
the gumption to do the same." Cryptic dodge of her questions. And how did he know Pike's name? Just how closely
had he been watching and eavesdropping? And for how
long? "The guy in the green sedan back there pulled up
and started watching your shop—waiting for you to leave,
maybe—as soon as the cops cleared out. Couldn't get a
clear look at the driver without giving away my position."

Giving himself away to whom? The driver or the cops?

"I did get a license number you can hand over to the
K-9 Corps there. Tell him you saw the guy watching your
place and you want to see if you can get an ID." He nodded
toward her shop across the street. "Did the suits give you
any idea why someone wanted to hurt you? Why they'd
still be following you?"

"What?" She glanced down at the scrap of paper he
pressed into her hand and read the make and model of
the green car, as well as the plate number scribbled there.
The man was thorough as well as observant. Shaking her
head, she crumpled the note in her fist and tipped her
chin, looking beyond the forbidding angles of his face to
meet his cool blue glare. "I don't understand you. You've
been here this whole time? Hiding out and watching this
nightmare? Are you afraid of the police? Have you done
something wrong? Did I say something that offended you?

I know I screamed at you when we first met, but I was under a little bit of stress. You startled me."

"No. I frightened you. It's part of my charm," he added in a self-mocking tone. "I'm used to it."

Robin bit down on the urge to argue her point. One look into those craggy, distorted features and she knew he wasn't exaggerating. It wasn't a handsome face. There was no friendly vibe here. Still, there'd been other things she'd noticed—his strength, his protective nature, his willingness to help a stranger in trouble—that she'd been attracted to, that she'd longed for tonight. "I'd hoped you'd stay with me. I needed you."

"You don't know me, lady. I'm not what you need."

"It's Robin, remember? And you have no idea what I needed tonight. I needed to feel safe. I needed to believe that no harm would come to my daughter. I needed an anchor in the middle of all that chaos. You said you'd stay."

"I said I'd stay until the cops showed up. I kept my word."

"You kept…?" She tapped the fist that held the paper against his shoulder, knowing she couldn't be so unkind—or foolish—to really vent her frustration against him. "The only time I felt safe tonight was when you were with us. I felt like somebody had my back so I didn't have to be afraid for a few minutes and I could think straight."

Lonergan shook his head. "I can't be that guy for you."

And yet he had been. "You're right. I don't know much about you. I don't know where you're from or what you've done. But tonight, you were everything Emma and I needed. *That's* the man I know. *That's* the man I expect you to be."

"You're welcome to your expectations, lady."

"Robin," she corrected, irritated with his adamant refusal to be civil. "Are you ever going to have the courtesy to tell me your first name?"

"I don't do niceties. Small talk isn't my thing."

"No. Strangling masked men, lurking in the shadows and being stubborn is your thing. At least have the good sense to get out of the rain." She retreated to the door, unsure whether she was inviting him in or urging him to leave.

"I will. Now that I know you're safe. Don't go out at night by yourself again. Especially with the kid. She'll distract your attention and slow you down."

"I'll do whatever is necessary to protect my daughter."

"Exactly." He moved a single step forward, filling up her personal space, perhaps trying to frighten her again, perhaps succeeding. "You won't do her any good if someone takes you out."

"Takes me out?

"I'm not talking about a date."

She knew what he'd meant. Why go to that dark, morbid place? What kind of man thought like this? In terms of basic survival. Black and white. Good and evil. Robin didn't know whether to fear this beast of a man or pity him. "Who are you, Mr. Lonergan?"

His voice dropped to a low and husky timbre that skittered across her ear drums and pricked each nerve into a heightened awareness of his heat and size and scent. "A guy with a knack for showing up in the wrong place at the wrong time."

Her own voice squeezed from her throat. "From my perspective, you entered my life at exactly the right time."

He shook his head. "I'm not *in* your life, lady."

Robin called him on his determined effort to deny any connection between them, whatever it might be. "Then why did you wait around for five hours to make sure I got safely to my destination?"

Lonergan braced his hand on the door frame behind her and leaned in. Robin sucked in her breath and flattened her back against the glass, feeling the heat from his body filling up the narrow space between them. He dipped his head, bringing that square, scarred jaw to within inches of her temple, forcing her to tilt her eyes to keep track of the intention in his grim expression. His hungry gaze dropped to her mouth and Robin thought he was going to close the distance and kiss her.

She held her breath in a mixture of anticipation and shock at just how badly she wanted to sample his kiss. A clear rivulet of rain dripped from tip of his nose onto her cheek. The cool drop sizzled against her skin and she gasped as if he'd physically touched her. "Let's just say I'm making sure my conscience is clear. I don't like to leave a job half done."

"You've done your job," she whispered. "I owe you so much. My life. Emma's life. What can I do to thank you?"

He leaned in another fraction of an inch and smoothed a wet lock of hair away from her eyes. His blunt fingers traced the wavy tendril against her scalp. His lips parted and his coffee-scented breath tickled her cheek. She was vaguely aware of his chest expanding and contracting at a more rapid pace.

That was what he wanted? A kiss? Closeness? To act on this charged energy arcing between them? Maybe a guy with that face and those scars didn't get much play with women, and he simply wanted sex. Certainly, his brusque personality wouldn't charm much feminine softness into his life. And yet, she was considering giving him exactly what those crystal blue eyes were asking for. The man was a virtual stranger. She was a smart, responsible woman.

Should she be this eager to reward him with a kiss? With something more?

Robin's hand somehow wound up on the masculine swell of his chest. She was bracing herself, curling her fingers into the wet cloth and solid muscle, holding on for what was sure to be a kiss unlike any other she'd experienced. Lonergan tunneled his fingers into her hair, tugging the wet strands and clasping the nape of her neck just a little too roughly.

"It's okay," she whispered, sensing his hesitation as much as his desire. "I'm okay with this."

Her eyes drifted shut and she stretched up to meet him. But just as she thought he'd touch his lips to hers, he muttered an oath. "I can't do this." He released her entirely and backed away. "You won't see me again, Robin."

Her eyes opened to see him striding away. He swiped a hand over his face and never looked back.

The emotional roller coaster of this long, sleepless night shook through her and left her knees wobbly enough that she had to cling to the bricks for support. "Yes, you will," she called after him, finding her voice and gaining strength. "I'm a determined woman. I repay my debts, Mr.... What the hell is your first name, anyway?"

But he disappeared around the fence, and the night and the rain swallowed him up.

Robin stared into the darkness, willing the sexy, frustrating, mysterious apparition to reappear. Willing her fascination with the man to stop pounding through her blood. After a minute of standing in the rain, feeling as empty and alone as she'd been before bringing Emma into her life, Robin had no choice but to go inside, bolt the doors behind her and trudge upstairs to claim whatever sleep she could.

Chapter Five

Seriously?

Ghost Rescuer Saves RRR's Latest Victim

Jake set down his mug of coffee and spread the newspaper open across the top of his kitchen table.

"Ghost Rescuer," he muttered, zeroing in on reporter Gabriel Knight's latest article in the *Kansas City Journal.* "According to one eyewitness, the unknown hero appeared 'like a ghost from the shadows.'" Jake crumpled the edge of the paper in his fist. "What eyewitness?"

The only people who'd been there last night had been an infant who couldn't talk and the blitz attacker who certainly wouldn't want Kansas City's top crime reporter covering his activities. That left the stubborn, dark-haired victim, Robin Carter, to blab about how he'd helped her. Some thanks.

"What are you doing to me, lady?" He didn't need this kind of publicity. He didn't need publicity, period. Getting featured in the newspaper worked against the whole idea of hiding out from the nightmares Jake suspected were all too real.

He swallowed the last of his tepid coffee and read the article from beginning to end. "Ah, hell."

At least she hadn't mentioned his name. But *big, scarred face* and *man who likes his privacy* were all apt descriptors that could lead anyone observant enough right to him.

He skimmed over Knight's claims that the Ghost Rescuer had done what KCPD had been unable to do for over a year now—stop the Rose Red Rapist. The women of Kansas City could breathe a little easier knowing someone like him lurked in the shadows, watching over them, waiting to save the day. He was making Jake out to be some kind of folk hero. This reporter clearly had a beef with the police department, but Jake wasn't about to sacrifice his anonymity to become a front-page news story in which Gabriel Knight could vent his anger and disappointment.

Jake glanced behind him at the closet where his go-bag, with all those IDs and his weapons cache, was stored. A man like…whoever he was…had a strong aversion to publicity, even good press.

Would whoever had cut his face, burned his skin and put a bullet in his head see this article and come back to finish the job? Would word of an anonymous hero lurking in the alleyways of Kansas City reach one of those Central American countries stamped on those fake passports? Or had he already taken out the people who'd done this to him? Was there enough detail in this article to get the attention of a law-enforcement agency that had him on their most-wanted list?

"Hell." Jake knocked the chair backward as he stood up abruptly, sending the shirt he hadn't yet put on tumbling to the floor. He wadded the newspaper in his fists and tossed it across the apartment. He could damn well be sure the local cops would be keeping an eye out for him now. And he worked in a cop bar! Great place to blend in and eavesdrop on official business, giving him a heads up on any investigation that might lead back to him. Bad place to be if KCPD had an actual suspect description that matched his face.

"You're ruining my life, Robin Carter." He stalked across the apartment to the fire escape window and pushed it open so he could sit on the ledge and breathe in several lungfuls of the storm-scrubbed morning air.

He didn't want to move on. He'd learned how to be good at leaving. He could move quickly and silently and be gone before anyone knew it.

But he liked Kansas City. He didn't know if he'd grown up a city boy or a country bumpkin, but he liked the mix of urban amenities and small-town sensibilities he'd found here. He could lose himself in a big city crowd or take a bus and be out in the wide-open countryside in thirty minutes. He couldn't remember if he was a Southerner or a Midwesterner or even an American, but he felt at home here. As at home as a man with no connections could be, at any rate.

And what about those Carter girls? Jake looked down at the newsprint stains on his rough, nicked-up hands. These were hands that were used for fighting, heavy lifting, killing. And yet he could still feel the silky strength of Robin Carter's wet, wavy hair tangled in his fingers. He could still remember how warm and fragile tiny Emma had felt sleeping in his hands and snuggling against his chest. The sensations had been as vivid and unfamiliar as they'd been strangely addictive.

Probably because he had no woman in his life. He had no family he remembered. He was starved for human contact. But he'd made a point of denying himself those things so there'd be no attachments if he had to leave, no regrets if something happened to a lover he cared about because of who he used to be. His face and personality made it easy to keep people away.

But that whole gotta-save-the-innocents hang-up of his had gotten him into trouble last night. Robin and Emma Carter were a family, in and of themselves. There was no man to protect them, no husband or boyfriend or daddy they'd called on for help. They'd needed him. *Him*. A pretty woman with that much sass and a beautiful baby should have someone taking care of them. They shouldn't be alone to fight against would-be rapists or whatever that mess had been about last night.

Showing up once he could write off as self-preservation—he didn't need any more guilt and what-ifs in his life. If he knew something was wrong, and he could do something about it, he needed to do it.

But showing up twice? Yeah, he'd been suspicious of the guy watching Robin's shop. Maybe it had been this Gabriel Knight; maybe that's how he'd gotten this story. But what had Jake been thinking? Hiding in the rain, waiting to catch her alone. Had he really just needed to see that she got safely home for the night? Or had he been hoping for something more? Had he really thought she'd let him kiss her? Thanks for the rescue, now pay up?

Jake closed his eyes and leaned back against the windowsill. He evaluated his options. Leave town before the Ghost Rescuer became any more of a buzz word. Leave a decent job with a fair boss who didn't ask questions. Leave the woman and baby who'd gotten under his skin and into his head in just a few short hours.

Or did he stay and trust that his covert skills could keep him out of any more newspapers? Stay and blend back into the shadows so he wouldn't show up as someone suspicious on KCPD's radar? Stay and pretend he wasn't worried about the single mom and daughter combo who'd been thrust into a world of violence with no one to protect them?

Could he remain in K.C. and not have a thing to do with Robin and Emma Carter?

None of those questions got answered. He might not remember his name, but he remembered the training that had kept him alive. Jake shifted his thoughts firmly to the present. There were eyes on him. Right now. He could feel someone was watching him, perched on the window ledge five stories above the street.

Without changing his body posture Jake opened his eyes and scanned the windows across the street. Unlived in or empty because the occupants had gone to work. He dropped his gaze to the street below to check out parked cars and moving traffic. Alleys? Clear. Rooftops? Clear.

And then he spotted the man in the trilby hat, leaning against the newsstand at the corner. He held a newspaper up as if he was reading it. The brim of the hat obscured his face, but it tipped up at least twice, indicating the man was looking up. At Jake.

Was he reading about the Ghost Rescuer in the *Journal,* and Jake's silver-white hair had stood out against the black fire escape and caught his eye? Or was there something more personal, more sinister about the man's curiosity?

Stretching his arms in a mock show of casual unawareness, Jake got up and closed the window. He jogged to the kitchen sink to wash his hands and splash water on his face and neck before pulling on a clean shirt and slipping out of the apartment to get a better look at just who might be fool enough to spy on him.

ROBIN PATTED EMMA'S bottom as the baby cooed contentedly in the sling Robin wore over her uninjured shoulder. Holding her daughter close to her chest, Robin leaned over the counter and turned to another page in the flower arrangement catalog.

She pointed to one of the pictures, hoping the middle-aged couple she was waiting on would see a little reason. "I could hang smaller sprays on each of the church pews if you want more color. But I think adding garland along the railing will make it look like the holidays, not a renewal of your wedding vows."

"Hmm." Chloe Vanderham tapped her hot-pink lacquered fingernail against the image of pastel spring flowers and sighed again. Then she turned to the balding man checking an app on his smart phone beside her. "What do you think, Paul?"

"That's fine." He raised his head without pulling his gaze from the phone. "Whatever you want, darlin'. This is my gift to you."

Chloe wrapped those shiny nails around her husband's chin and demanded his full attention. "This is supposed to be a celebration of *our* twentieth anniversary, Paul. Not just mine." She turned his face toward the catalog. "I like this arrangement. But with red roses. Long-stemmed ones spilling down like a waterfall at the front of the church."

"Do you really think red is appropriate, given the recent events in town?" He pulled her fingers from his jaw and gave them a placating kiss before releasing her. "You look so lovely in pink."

The suggestion didn't seem to please her. Robin thought she might even have heard the stamping of a platformed heel. "I had red at our first wedding. I'm not going to let that awful man dictate how I celebrate my own anniversary. I won't have it."

With his patience already overtaxed by coming to the shop with his wife in the first place, Paul made no effort to mask his frustration. He tucked his phone inside his suit jacket and pleaded to Robin. "Bail me out here, please."

Silently forgiving them for not knowing she might have

been the most recent victim of the Rose Red Rapist's attacks, Robin searched for a resolution that would keep these two from walking out the door in an angry huff. She'd built a successful company out of giving customers what they wanted. Mediating disputes like this one, and helping her clients reach a decision, was all part of the business. Even if it was a chore to deal with when she'd rather be napping, looking at her accounting reports with fresh eyes or finding answers to the mysteries that lingered from last night. Who had attacked her? Why? Who was Lonergan? Why had he almost kissed her? Why had she been so foolishly ready to kiss him back?

Fighting back the curious heat that warmed her skin, Robin offered both the Vanderhams a reassuring smile. "Chloe, you said your original bouquet had red roses in it?"

"Yes. Red roses and white carnations."

"Why don't we re-create that bouquet and feature the red there? That would draw everyone's attention to you, especially if we use softer tones and smaller arrangements for the decorations." Plus, she wouldn't risk over ordering stock and having a supply of the bloodred flowers on hand to tempt the infamous rapist.

Paul winked his gratitude and Chloe smiled. "You are a woman of excellent taste, Robin."

"I try."

Chloe twirled the cluster of diamonds and white gold on her ring finger. "I know it's short notice, with the ceremony just a week away, but can you get everything ready?"

"I'll need to check with my vendors to make sure we have what we need available. But at this time of year, it shouldn't be an issue. And my staff works quickly once we have the proper materials." She called to the blonde assistant stocking hydrangea bunches in the refrigerated display case. "Hey, Shirley. Would you run to the back and see if Leon has left to make his deliveries yet? If he's still here, ask him to bring me the stock manifest for the flowers that came in this morning."

"Will do."

Shirley wiped her hands on her smock and exited through the swinging doors while Robin pulled up the Vanderhams' order on her computer screen. Emma shifted in the sling, blowing bubbles through her tiny bowed lips and drawing Robin's attention down to the contented baby smiling up at her. "You're such a good girl," she praised, adding baby talk sound effects that made Emma gurgle and squiggle even more. Robin wiped the bubbles from her baby's lips and pressed a kiss to her velvety brown hair. "Did you want to get into your swing to see the world? It's not fair that you got seven hours of sleep while Mommy only got two." Emma started suckling on Robin's finger and she nearly forgot about everyone else in the shop. "Ready for an afternoon snack, are we?"

The bell hanging over the front door jingled. Reluctantly, Robin pulled her attention away from Emma to greet the new customer.

Her one-time beau—the man she'd bought this very shop from after his company had renovated the building—Brian Elliott, walked in, circled the counter, kissed her cheek and wrapped her in a hug. Instinctively, Robin's arms curled around Emma, protecting her from being crushed between them. "Oh, God, sweetheart, are you okay?"

She took note of his expensive cologne and the concern that lined his dark eyes. "I'm fine, Brian," she reassured him, reaching one arm around his crisp gabardine suit to pat his back. "Just a few bruises."

"That sick man was lying in wait for you? You should have called me as soon as this happened," he insisted.

"In the middle of the night?"

"You know I still care about you."

"There's nothing you could have done. The police came. I answered their questions. Then we went across the street and spent the night at Hope's."

She left out the juicy bits about someone toppling Emma's car seat, strangers watching her shop and a ghost saving the day and rousing an unfamiliar, dangerously potent desire inside her.

Unlike her bland "nope, nothing" firing anywhere in her system in response to Brian's hug.

If the initial embrace had been awkward, the end of it was even more so. Brian must have realized how she shielded the baby between them and he sucked in his stomach and arched his back, breaking contact with Emma before he pulled his arms from Robin. He plucked the front edge of the sling between his thumb and forefinger and pulled it up around Emma, even as she buzzed her lips and reached for one of the buttons on his jacket. "Should she be here?"

Ah, yes. One of the reasons they'd broken up—Brian's aversion to starting a family.

Robin reached inside the sling to let Emma's delicate, grasping fingers grab hold of one of hers, silently apologizing for the rejection. Brian was a wealthy workaholic. That he'd taken time out of his busy schedule to pay her a visit was his way of saying he still cared. Too bad that caring didn't extend to her daughter. "What are you doing here, Brian?"

He unrolled the newspaper he clutched in his hand and slapped it on the counter. "I came as soon as I read this. I'm disgusted with Knight's coverage of the task force investigation. Pure publicity stunt if you ask me. At least the *Journal* had the decency not to run any pictures." He reached out to touch the scrape along her jaw and she quickly averted her head to avoid the contact.

"Not very flattering, is it?" Robin had seen the small headline near the bottom of the front page. *Local Woman Survives Assault.* It was weird to see herself and the events of last night described in such impersonal detail. She'd read the short article over coffee with Hope this morning, and had cringed at seeing her name linked to a possible attack by the Rose Red Rapist. And even though they hadn't mentioned Emma by name, she'd already put in a call to the paper complaining about the reporter's emphasis on her being a single mother and how her child could have been left abandoned to the elements by a criminal with no moral regard for the minor's safety. The only positive was Gabriel Knight's mention of the Ghost Rescuer who'd come to her assistance and how the man should be decorated for his bravery.

"He said you were beaten. You could have died."

"Mr. Knight made it sound worse than it was," Robin lied, trying to placate the concern that steeled Brian's handsome features and snagged the Vanderhams' interest.

"You should let me hire security for this place," Brian offered.

"Why? This is my shop, not yours. Whatever happens here is my responsibility."

"But a team of bodyguards—"

"—would drive away business."

"This isn't the time to assert your independence, Robin. The Rose Red Rapist isn't a man you want to take chances with."

Needing to change the subject before the fear and helplessness she'd felt last night grabbed hold of her again,

Robin turned to introduce everyone. "Brian Elliott, this is Paul and Chloe Vanderham. They're longtime customers here."

"We've done business together before." Brian reached across the counter to shake hands with Paul. Making himself at home in her workspace, Brian helped himself to a paper towel from under the counter and wiped the black newsprint from his hands before extending a hand to Paul's wife. "Chloe, how are you?"

"Wonderful, as always. Wonderful to see you, too." The platinum blonde picked up the newspaper, then looked at Robin. "This is you? I felt so sorry for the woman in this article. And that man who came out of nowhere to rescue you? Gabe Knight made it sound like a fairy tale."

Um, no.

Perhaps the three glares directed her way finally got through Chloe's heartless rambling. She arched her brows in a pitying frown. "Are you all right? Should you be at work today?"

Brian answered before she could. "No, she shouldn't."

Okay. Another reason why she and Brian hadn't worked. She could speak for herself. "I'm not going to let that man turn me into a recluse. I have to earn a living to support Emma. Besides, staying busy helps keep my mind occupied."

She didn't need the particular distraction these three provided, though, as the conversation veered off into a discussion of the *Kansas City Journal*'s editor-in-chief, Mara Boyd-Elliott.

Paul glanced at the paper over his wife's shoulder. "Mara is doing a fine job of running the *Journal* in her father's place. I miss old Jared Boyd, though. He was a man who didn't mince words. I always enjoyed reading his editorials." Brian bristled at the mention of his ex-wife. "Do you two still keep in touch?"

"My father-in-law is dead."

"Ex-father-in-law," Paul corrected, continuing the conversation as cluelessly as Chloe had, as if a deceased family member and divorced wife were better topics than Robin's assault. "I meant Mara, of course. Do you keep in touch with her?"

"Only regarding legal issues that come up, or to discuss an article for the paper."

"That's right. She's commissioned some glowing reviews and spectacular pictures of your downtown renovation project in the paper's Kansas City Living section." Paul went on, as oblivious to the discomfort he was causing as he'd been to his wife's desire to share the ceremony planning experience with him. "I'll bet Mara still does as much to benefit your business as she did when she was your wife."

Robin could feel the tension radiating off Brian beside her. "Paul—"

"You wanted to see me, Ms. Carter?" Leon Hundley pushed through the swinging doors, thankfully interrupting the awkward conversation.

"Yes, Leon, thank you." Robin's greeting was more effusive than the friendly professionalism she normally treated her employees with. Although, she was taken aback for a moment when she saw the turtleneck the younger man was wearing beneath his green uniform shirt. Now that last night's thunderstorm had blown past, the June afternoon had turned sunny and humid. "Aren't you hot in that?

He shrugged his wiry shoulders. "You know how cold it gets in the fridge room, ma'am."

"I suppose." She herself kept an old sweater in her office for when she had to work in the fridge room for any length of time. Well, if he could tolerate the humidity, his discomfort wasn't her concern. "I need to see the stock manifest from the flowers you picked up this morning."

Leon pawed at his collar, as if the turtleneck felt as itchy and out of season as it looked. "I don't have that list. I turned it over to Mark after I unloaded everything. We've been doing it like that for a while now since you've been gone. I just turn the paperwork over to him."

Mark Riggins was her assistant manager, and had run the shop in her absence. Although an alarm bell went off in her head at the change in store procedure coinciding with the accounting discrepancies, she trusted Mark. From what she knew of his flamboyant personality, she wouldn't think bookkeeping would be his favorite thing. Maybe he'd just made some honest mistakes—deliveries that hadn't been entered, an order he forgot to record payment on. When the stream of customers died down, she could pull him aside and ask him about the books. "I guess I need to talk to Mark, then." Leon nodded and started to walk away, but Robin stopped him. "So what did the market look like this morning? Were there shortages of anything I ordered?"

He scratched at his short brown hair, as though replaying his morning errands in his head. "Yeah. They were having shipping issues with some of the hothouse flowers. Orchids and birds-of-paradise. That kind of stuff."

Chloe piped up. "Ooh. Birds-of-paradise would be beautiful standing up on the altar, wouldn't they, Paul?"

Robin averted her head in case she rolled her eyes. Hadn't the woman just heard there was a shortage of that particular flower? And did she really think the exotic orange flower would look good with anything else she'd picked out today? Once she had her tongue and patience firmly in check, Robin turned to Chloe. "Don't worry. There will be plenty of roses, I'm sure."

"Yes, ma'am. There always is." Leon had always happier driving the truck than interacting with customers in the shop. He shifted on his booted feet and tugged at his collar again. "Is that all, Ms. Carter? I need to get those arrangements delivered to the hospitals before closing time."

"Sure, Leon. You run along. Oh." She tugged on his sleeve to catch him before her left. "Tomorrow morning, bring the stock manifests to me. I'll explain the change to Mark."

His wiry shoulders lifted in an irritated sigh. "Yes, ma'am."

When he left, Robin wished she could go with him because Brian was at her side again, reaching for her hand. "Is there anything I can do for you? Anything you need? You could stay a few days at the penthouse—let my staff wait on you so you can relax."

"I prefer my own home, thanks."

Chloe asked another question about the exotic flowers. Paul pulled out his cell phone and Robin considered pulling out her hair. But her patience was given a respite by the ringing of the telephone. She quickly turned to the back wall and picked up the receiver before the second ring. "Hello. Robin's Nest Floral. This is Robin, may I help you?"

"Ms. Carter?" The deep tone was brusque, and she instantly knew this wasn't a customer. "Spencer Montgomery here. Can you talk?"

"Sure, I… Just a second. I'd like to get to someplace more private." She covered the mouthpiece and stuck her head through the swinging doors and shouted to the back rooms. "Mark? I need you up front." Then she turned to the people demanding her attention. "Mark is my top designer, Chloe. He'll finish taking your order." The phone's long cord followed behind her as she stretched up on tiptoe and kissed Brian's cheek. "Thank you for stopping by. But this is an important call I need to take. I'm sure you understand."

Although he didn't look terribly pleased by the dismissal, Brian kissed her cheek in return. Robin idly noted that there was not one flicker of erotic heat at the skin to skin contact, unlike that dangerous almost-kiss that had happened between her and Lonergan last night. Maybe she'd dated too many tailored suits like Brian Elliott over the years, and that was why someone as coarse and earthy as her rescuer seemed so appealing. Then again, maybe Chloe wasn't too far off in her "fairy tale" description of last night's rescue, after all, and Robin was succumbing to a little adolescent hero worship.

"Take care," said Brian, as coolly articulate and handsome as Lonergan was not. "Call if you need anything."

"I will." She placed the detective on hold and hurried down the hallway to her office.

En route, she ran into Mark Riggins, smoothing his store apron over his striped shirt and khakis. "What's the emergency?" he asked. "Leon said you were upset with him."

"I wasn't upset." Robin frowned, anxious to get to the phone, anxious to explain her suspicions to Mark, just... anxious. "I asked him a few questions. I wasn't accusing anyone of anything."

His dark eyes narrowed. "Accusing?"

Robin groaned with impatience. "I asked him about the stock and whether we've been getting all the supplies we've ordered. He said he's been funneling all that through you and didn't seem to know the details."

Mark made a little protesting noise and propped his

hands on his hips. "Leon is a sweet young man who excels at driving the van and doing manual labor. But he's no brain surgeon. I asked him to turn over all the paperwork to me because he was making a mess of it. If you have a problem with that, then you need to talk to me."

"Let's make an appointment and do that. Right now I need to take a phone call from KCPD."

"About last night?" Robin nodded and Mark's affronted stance melted away. He clapped his hands together. "That's too frightening for me to even contemplate—you being hurt like that. And poor Emma. What do you need me to do? Are we overrun with customers?"

She reached up to straighten the bow tie he wore and patted his shoulder. "No. Just one who has a ton of money to spend and can't make a decision. And I really need to take that call."

"A ton of money—my favorite kind of client." Mark fluffed his fingers through his curly brown hair and winked. "You deal with the police—I'll help the customers spend their money."

"Thank you. Owe you."

"Always happy to do a girl a favor." He burst through the doors with the flourish of a Broadway dance number and took over the appointment with the Vanderhams. "I'm Mark. Now what can I do for you, pretty lady?"

Knowing Mark could match Chloe Vanderham's divalicious personality, Robin closed the office door behind her. She quickly pulled the baby sling off her shoulder and lay Emma in her bassinet before picking up the extension. "Detective Montgomery? Sorry for the wait. Has something happened? Did you find the man who attacked me?"

"Not yet. But I think we found your Mr. Lonergan."

Robin wedged the phone between her ear and shoulder

so she could assemble a small bottle of formula for Emma while they talked. "Do you have a name? An address?"

"He goes by Jake."

Jake. It fit. Manly and to the point. Finally, she had a name for the hero who'd saved her life and Emma's. But wait a minute. Even as the news elated her, Robin frowned. "Goes by?"

Spencer Montgomery released a telling sigh. "There's no record of him in the DMV database."

"You mean he doesn't drive?"

"I mean the name is bogus. It's not like his license was taken away for DUIs or an accident. He doesn't exist. I haven't even found any IRS records on him."

The math wasn't hard to do. "That doesn't make sense. He's in his late thirties, maybe forty. And he's no bum. He has to have had a job and paid taxes for twenty years or so."

"Not according to my sources. No trackable history and he skips out before we can talk to him? Both are red flags in my book. Be careful with this man, Ms. Carter."

Robin sank down into the chair behind her desk. But he hadn't skipped out. Lonergan, make that *Jake* Lonergan, had been watching over her all night long. "Maybe he legally changed his name," she theorized.

"There'd be a paper trail," the detective explained. "This guy is way off the grid. My next step is to widen the search to Interpol because I can't locate official American records on him anywhere."

"Then how did you find him?"

"My partner, Nick, has good instincts about people. And he never forgets a face."

"Detective Fensom knows him?" How could that be? Why would Lonergan avoid the cops if they were friends? Unless that familiarity with her mystery man meant they

weren't? Robin shot to her feet again, shaking the mea-
sured formula powder and bottled water together with
more vigor than usual. "Do you think he's a criminal? Because he wasn't last night. He did a good deed. A great one
as far as I'm concerned. I don't want you to punish him."

"Relax." Spencer Montgomery's tone sounded straight-
forward, taking the edge off her defensive anger, even if
she didn't necessarily think he'd agreed to her demand.
"We just want to ask him some questions. We haven't approached him yet—we're not completely sure this is the
right guy. We'd like a second opinion."

"Do you need me to come down to the police station
to identify him?"

"Not exactly."

Robin groaned her frustration as one mystery com-
pounded another. "Detective Montgomery, I thought you
and I agreed we both like straight answers."

"We did. I'm trying to spare you some stress and disappointment if this isn't the guy."

"I can handle stress and disappointment, Detective. I
want to see this Jake Lonergan your partner found."

"Do you know where the Shamrock Bar is?"

Jake Lonergan hung out in bars? He was secretive, yes.
But he hadn't struck her as the kind of guy who'd waste his
time like that. "It's around the corner, a couple of blocks
from my shop. You want me to meet you there?"

"If you don't mind. You can get a look at our suspect…
er, person of interest there and see if he's your guy."

Robin hadn't missed the detective's slip. "He's not the
man who attacked me," she reiterated, getting the idea
it was up to her to prove that. "I can be there in twenty
minutes."

Torn between anticipation and anxiety at the chance to
see if Detectives Montgomery and Fensom had tracked

down the right Lonergan, Robin sat down for ten minutes to give Emma the bottle she needed. Then she burped her and changed her diaper before wasting another five minutes trying to track down Emma's yellow hat. "Where is it?" She emptied out the contents of Emma's bag and the hamper. "Never mind."

Ignoring the phone ringing on her desk and from every extension in the front and back of the shop, she pulled out a shopping bag from a weekend excursion to the Plaza and opened up a new outfit she'd bought for Emma's six-month picture. She left the flowered shirt and overalls in the bag and tied the matching sun hat onto Emma's head. "Happy early birthday, sweetie. It clashes a little, but it'll do."

She was packing the stroller and heading out when Mark stuck his head through the swinging doors. "Robin? Phone." He dropped his voice to a whisper. "I think it's one of those reporters."

"Would you tell him to…" Wait. If that was Gabriel Knight calling back about his news article, then she needed to have a discussion that made it clear that any mention of her daughter was off limits in any follow-up stories. "Never mind. I'll take it in my office."

By the time Robin had rolled the stroller back to her desk, Mark had transferred the call to her private line. She picked up the phone. "This is Robin Carter." Several seconds of answering silence passed and she checked the lighted line on the phone to make sure they were still connected. "Hello? Is this Mr. Knight?"

She heard a sharp intake of breath before a woman's voice spoke. "You don't deserve to have that baby."

A brief moment of confusion at the unexpected accusation was replaced by the chill that ran down her spine. "Who is this?"

"You aren't her real mother. Her real mother wouldn't put her in harm's way like you did. She could have died."

The words were slightly slurred, yet frighteningly articulate. A chill flowed through Robin's body, sapped her strength. She obeyed the sudden weakness in her knees and sank to the floor beside the stroller—needing to see Emma's bright blue eyes, needing to hear the soft, rhythmic sucking of her thumb, needing to touch the precious reality of her miracle baby.

"I'm on my way to talk to the police right now," she warned, sounding braver than the fearful knot in her chest felt. "Who are you? Don't you dare speak to me about my daughter."

"*Your* daughter?" The woman laughed. "I know the truth about that baby. You don't deserve her. He should have killed you when he had the chance."

"Who are you? Why are you saying these hateful things? What do you want?"

Robin jumped at the loud click that ended the call.

The first thing she did was pick up Emma and hug her tightly to her chest, rocking her back and forth and pressing a kiss to each cheek, taking strength from the scents that had become as familiar to her as breathing. "You *are* my daughter," she vowed, needing to hear the words herself as much as she wanted to reassure the infant who couldn't understand those words yet. "I'm not leaving you. I'm not letting anyone take you from me."

The second thing she did was strap Emma back into her stroller and head out the front door, turning up the sidewalk toward the Shamrock Bar. Detective Montgomery would want to hear about the call, right? That CSI last night had said the accomplice who cleaned up after the Rose Red Rapist's attacks was a woman. Were those vile threats related to the assault? Even if the caller was just some crank drunk who'd been reading the morning paper, the message was disturbing.

Robin wasn't ashamed to admit that her sense of independence and security had been rattled again. She needed to feel safe.

She needed to find Jake.

Chapter Six

Jake shrugged into his insulated gloves and lifted the two cases of bottled beer. The strain on his muscles was as welcome a distraction as the blast of cold air from the walk-in fridge had been.

He'd had a fitful morning of sleep, plagued by images of Robin Carter soaked to the skin, tearing at his clothes while he tangled his fingers in her soft, sable-brown hair and plundered those bewitching lips and other parts of her body with a hunger he hadn't indulged since the day he'd woken up without a past. The erotic dreams had been as disturbing as the violence that normally haunted his sleep, and had required a cold shower to wash most of them out of his head.

Plus, he hadn't been able to catch the guy in the trilby hat who'd been watching him. Either the guy had walked away before Jake could reach him, or he was really good at blending in with a crowd. As good as Jake was when he put his mind to it.

His snarly mood hadn't improved much at work, either. Instead of figuring out why the guy at the newsstand might be interested in him, Jake had been thinking about events he *could* remember, like the feel of Robin's long, lean body pressed against his side. He could recall the exact moment when the fear in her eyes had turned to trust. And he'd never forget her thrusting that baby girl into his arms. If the mama was a temptation he didn't need, then that infant with the big blue eyes and snuggling instincts was downright dangerous to his determination to fly solo through the shadows of the world.

The woman was pretty in that classy, PTA mom kind of way that meant she was more at home with a white-collar executive who drove a minivan and lived in the suburbs than with a...whatever he was. In the light of day, he'd like to think she was too skinny to entice a man with his baser tastes. But he'd seen the curves on that backside. He'd touched that soft, cool skin. How could he justify getting attached to anyone—a stubborn woman or a sweet little girl—if he didn't know who he was and what he had done? And if he thought his brain was screwed up now, what if the things he'd done came back with a vengeance and hurt the people he cared about?

"Care about," Jake sneered. What a ludicrous idea to think he'd formed any kind of attachment to the Carter girls in the short span of hours he'd known them. Swearing at his own weakness for even considering such a thing, he hit the insulated door's release handle and carried his load through the back hallway into the front of the Shamrock Bar.

He pushed through the swinging door behind the polished walnut bar and froze. *Speak of the devil.* No, not the devil—more like a pair of angels walking through the front door. Robin Carter looked pretty nice all dried off, too.

Jake took a breath, recovering from a jolt of eager recognition, and thumped the cases down on top of the bar. "What are you doing here?"

The armed suit who'd held the door open for Robin and the kid in the stroller moved in before she could speak and flashed his badge. "Spencer Montgomery, KCPD. You're Jake Lonergan?"

For now. "Yeah."

Robin pushed the stroller right up to the barstools. "That's him, Detective."

So she'd brought the cops right to him, served up his name and face on a platter despite every effort to disappear from her life. *Thanks for nothin', honey*. His effort to glare Robin Carter back out the door made her pull her shoulders back and tip her chin. Oh, yeah. She was quivering in those running shoes she wore, but she refused to be intimidated.

"Hello, Jake."

"I don't do the niceties, remember?" Jake pulled a box cutter from his apron pocket, sliced open the top crate and starting loading beer bottles into the cooler beneath the bar.

"I'd like to ask you a few questions," said the detective. "Namely, why would you flee the scene of a crime?"

Yeah. He was ignoring him, too.

"Jake?" Robin cleared the husky catch in her voice and spoke again. "It *is* Jake, isn't it? I told him you didn't run away—that you were there, watching over us, all night."

He tossed the empty box to the floor and proceeded to open and unload the second one. "I don't need you to defend me. Am I under some kind of suspicion, Officer?"

Before the detective could answer, the door swung open behind Jake, and Robbie Nichols, Jake's boss, carried out a freshly washed crate of beer mugs.

"Customers, already?" Robbie's Irish heritage was evident in both his accent and his jovial greeting. He set the glasses on the bar and grinned through his bushy black beard and mustache.

"No." The place was nearly deserted this early in the

evening, so there was no mistaking that Robin and the suit with the badge were here to see him.

"Friends of yours, then." The fact that Jake had never had one friend stop in for a visit didn't seem to faze Robbie. The burly Irishman stretched his arm across the bar to shake hands with the detective. "Spencer Montgomery—we don't see enough of you around here anymore."

The carrot top with Robin nodded. "Mr. Nichols. Since my partner got engaged, he'd rather take his fiancée out for drinks after work than come here with me. Go figure."

Robbie chuckled. "So it's a date then?"

"No."

"No."

"No." Jake, Robin and the detective all answered in unison.

Seeming oblivious to the tension in the room, Robbie lifted the gate at the end of the bar and circled around to squat down beside the stroller. "And who might this little beauty be?"

He poked his fat finger into the stroller and laughed when Emma Carter batted at it and then latched on. He tilted his face to Robin. "I'm Robbie Nichols, the owner of this fine establishment. May I, Mrs....?"

"*Ms.* Carter. Robin." Jake watched a smile warm her face as she bent down to unhook the baby and pick her up. "This is Emma. She can hold up her head now, but you still want to make sure you support her."

A protective impulse, as instant as it was foreign, heated Jake's blood as he watched Robin place the baby in his boss's arms. "Be careful with her, Robbie."

Robbie waved off the warning and buzzed some motorboat noises that made Emma giggle and tug on his beard. "I know how to handle a wee babe like this. Don't I take care of my great-nephew just fine when Josie brings him in for a visit?"

Jake remembered how small and fragile Emma had felt in his hands. "Aaron's a boy and he can walk."

"He's one and a half. Still in diapers. He was this size once. Josie—my niece," he explained to Robin, who didn't seem to have any problem handing her baby off to men she'd just met, "trusts me with him."

"Yeah, well…be careful," Jake warned. The notion that it wasn't his place to warn anyone away from the little girl registered a moment too late.

Robin's eyes narrowed with a question for Jake before she smiled at Robbie again. "You handle her like a pro, Mr. Nichols."

"Robbie," he said, making both the Carter girls feel welcome.

While they spent a minute getting acquainted, and Jake tried to bury that troublesome penchant for rescuing damsels in distress by diving into his work, Detective Montgomery slid onto the green leather seat of a barstool and slyly voiced a comment. "Thanks for the tip on the license plate."

Jake stopped with his fists around the necks of two bottles and flashed an accusatory glance at Robin. Her cheeks flushed with rosy heat before she defended herself. "I didn't tell him you gave it to me."

Montgomery coolly eyeballed Jake and vice versa. He'd have to be careful around this perceptive cop if he wanted to maintain his anonymity as the strong, silent type who served beers and threw out drunks who disrupted the peace. The detective probably made a hell of a poker player in most circles, but Jake had known men like him before. He wasn't sure who or when, but he recognized a man who was a lot smarter and more aware than he let on. Maybe because Jake was that type of man himself.

He had to respect the kind of cop Montgomery was. But that also meant he had to work a little harder—or maybe play a little nicer—to stay off the detective's radar. "You have to include my name in that police report if I answer your questions?"

Montgomery's gray eyes were wary. "Any reason why I shouldn't?"

Jake placed the last of the beers in the cooler and ditched the box. Robin seemed to be holding her breath, waiting for his answer. He didn't want the perceptive detective to get too curious about him. Robin, either. "I'm just a guy who likes his privacy."

"Jake, I don't mean to intrude," Robin apologized, "but I asked Detective Montgomery to find you because I wanted to—"

"Ask your questions, Detective." She *wanted* something from him? Jake nipped that notion in the bud before he even acknowledged that he liked the idea of Robin Carter wanting something from him.

"Mr. Lonergan, what were you doing in the alley behind the Robin's Nest Floral Shop last night?" he asked.

"Walking." Jake ignored the expression on Robin's face—hurt? confusion? frustration?—and concentrated on what information he'd share with the detective. He pulled out the dishtowel hooked into the band of his apron and wiped down the bar.

"After midnight?"

"I got off work early and couldn't sleep."

"So you got up in the middle of the night and went for a walk in a thunderstorm?"

"I really couldn't sleep."

Despite his nod, Detective Montgomery didn't look

like he was buying Jake's excuse. The red-haired detective would make a worthy adversary. Or a solid ally. It was hard not to speculate on which Spencer Montgomery would have been if Jake had his memory back and knew what kind of man *he* was.

He moved to the glasses Robbie had brought in and finished drying them and putting them away. It was just as hard not to speculate about what kind of woman he'd been with before he'd been shot. Blonde? Brunette? Tough and street savvy? A no-strings-attached sex buddy? Or someone wholesome and trusting like the woman slipping him sly looks as she chatted with Robbie and played with the baby.

Maybe he'd been such an awful S.O.B. back then that he hadn't had any woman in his life. Shards of need and regret cut through the emptiness inside him. With no link to his past and no one in his current sham of a life, he understood loneliness the way most folks understood breathing. He didn't want to think he'd lived his whole life feeling this way. But if there was some good in his past, someone he'd been important to, then why hadn't they come to see him in the hospital? Why had none of the addresses in his stash led to a real home? Every lead had taken him to a warehouse or an empty lot. All the clues to his past life were fake except for the nightmares.

He had a feeling if there'd been anyone like Robin Carter in his life, she wouldn't have stopped searching until she'd tracked him down. Which was exactly what she'd done. Jake fisted his hand in the dishtowel and muttered a curse. Now *that* was irony. The thing he wanted most was the one thing he'd sworn he'd never let himself have.

"Did you see anyone in the neighborhood while you

were out walking?" Montgomery asked, interrupting his thoughts.

Jake pulled his hungry gaze away from the dark brown waves of Robin's hair that bounced around her face every time she laughed with Robbie or shook her head after reaching into her pocket to check her cell phone. "You want to know if I saw the guy who went after Ms. Carter."

"Yes."

Good. They were past subterfuge now and Jake gave a straight answer. "I didn't. I heard her whistle, heard her scream and went to check it out. The guy was average height. On the skinny side. He wore black coveralls and a stocking mask, and he ran fast. Didn't know much about fighting—probably why he had to ambush her with a baseball bat."

"You had the wherewithal to pull the attacker off Ms. Carter and subdue him, but you never looked at his face?"

"Seemed more important at the time to make sure she was still breathing." What was with the phone? Robin had checked her cell twice now that he'd seen. The easy explanation was that she was expecting an important call, but she had to reaffix the smile on her face each time she stuffed the cell back into her jeans and resumed her interest in Robbie's chatter.

Something was off. It wasn't his concern, though. It couldn't be.

Spencer Montgomery must have finally decided Jake wasn't going to be much help to his investigation. He pulled out his cell phone and set his notepad on top of the bar. "I'll run the plate through the DMV and see if we can get a hit on who was loitering outside the shop. Maybe he'll match your general description of Ms. Carter's attacker and we can bring him in for questioning." The detective slid one of his business cards across the bar. "If you think of anything else, call me."

With the interview over, Jake knew he should pick up the empty boxes and carry them out to the trash, giving Robin and the kid plenty of time to leave before he did something stupid like go over there and ask what was bugging her about her phone.

But he was a cursed man. Cursed to have amnesia. Cursed to look like the aftermath of a lost battle. Cursed to feel that compulsion to atone for the violence from his nightmares.

When he saw Robbie lifting Emma over his head and pretending she was an airplane, Jake dropped the boxes and charged around the end of the bar. It didn't matter that the baby was laughing from deep in her belly, or that Robin was carefully watching the ride through the air. Emma was too tiny, too pretty—too perfect—to risk her getting hurt.

"Stop!" Jake plucked the baby from his hands before Robbie sent her flying. "You'll break her."

Baby saved. Now what? He pulled Emma into his chest, keeping one arm beneath her bottom and leaning back a bit so she wouldn't fall. But she kept wiggling around, batting at his neck and bobbing in his grasp. It was like handling a squirming piece of blown glass. Two tiny fingers hooked into the side of his mouth while the other miniature hand brushed across the stubble of his jaw. She squealed in his ear.

"She's going to scratch herself," he mumbled awkwardly, afraid to close his mouth around her fingers. "I haven't shaved since last night."

"Jake, she's okay." Robin's smile probably meant his inexperience handling a baby amused her. But her hand on his arm softened the sting of overreacting and feeling out of his element. She guided his hand to the baby's back and pulled the clinging fingers from his mouth. "Babies like to feel different textures. Touch is a big part of how they learn."

They also didn't seem to care a whit for how big and ugly the man was behind those textures. Emma flashed him those sweet blue eyes and squealed with delight as she rubbed both tiny palms along his scarred jaw. Oh, man. He was screwed.

He wasn't the only one in the bar to notice that, either.

Robbie's gut shook as he laughed and winked at Jake. "I see how it is. The heart of the beast has been smitten by the wee beauty." He reached over to tickle the back of Emma's neck and then pat Jake on the arm. "I'll take the trash out for you and leave you be with your friends. You've got about twenty minutes before the first round of customers stops by after work." He had a wink for Robin, too. "Nice to meet you both. Now that I know we're practically neighbors, you come visit again, anytime."

"Nice to meet you." After Robbie had picked up the boxes and exited into the back hallway, Robin peeked around Jake's shoulder and confirmed that the detective was on the phone to someone at precinct headquarters. She had that determined tilt to her chin again when she looked at Jake. "Are you done talking with Detective Montgomery?"

The woman just wouldn't leave him alone and give him the chance to get her out of his head, would she.

"Didn't have much to say. Here." He leaned in and carefully handed Emma over, pulling away just as quickly as it took for him to know Robin had a good grip on her daughter. "You get her out of here. A bar is no place for a baby."

"I'll leave you alone if that's what you want. But I need to talk to you first. Will you listen?"

He wasn't getting rid of the Carter girls until he did, Jake suspected, so he reluctantly pointed to a booth away from the main bar. "I'll give you ten minutes."

"Robbie said we had twenty."

"I'll give you ten." Especially since his shirt now smelled faintly of baby, and he wanted to swap it out for a clean shirt he kept in his locker in the back room before he had to spend the entire night getting whiffs of the "wee beauty" who had somehow gotten under his skin.

At Robin's request, he retrieved the stroller and followed them over to the booth. With Emma propped up on her mother's shoulder, smiling at him the entire way, Jake had to wonder if the little minx knew she was casting a spell over him.

He'd let Robin have her say. But then he'd make it clear that helping her the night before had been a one-time thing. As far as he was concerned, their paths need never cross again.

Jake waited for Robin to strap Emma into the stroller at the end of the table, and pull out a set of colorful plastic keys for her to play with before they slipped into opposite sides of the booth. He leaned back, folded his arms over his chest and waited for Robin to start the conversation.

He had to give the woman credit for getting straight to the point. "I'd like to take you to dinner to thank you for what you did for us. Better yet, I'd like to fix you a meal. I'm guessing you're not a man who gets much home cooking."

Jake patted his stomach. "You don't think I eat?" So what if most of his meals came from a microwave or were takeout? It didn't mean he was starving. Or that he wanted to become a charity project for her. "You already said thank you. More than once."

She tucked one of those chin-length strands of hair behind her ear and breathed deeply, gearing up to try a different approach. "It doesn't seem like enough. You didn't just water my plants while I was on vacation—you saved our lives. I'd like to do something a little more tangible to express our gratitude. I think you'd be insulted if I offered you money—"

"I would."

"—and you don't strike me as a man who'd appreciate a big bouquet of flowers. Besides, up until thirty minutes ago, I had no idea where I'd have my man deliver it. I thought you'd appreciate something practical. You have to eat. I cook. Pretty well, I think. And I almost always fix more than…"

Robin stopped mid-sentence with a soft gasp and looked down. She pulled out her cell phone and Jake heard another, almost inaudible, gasp. She was doing it again—that little shake of the head, as though she was dismissing something unpleasant. She closed the phone in her fist and set it down in her lap, out of sight beneath the table.

"You need to answer that?" Jake asked, before she could resume the argument.

"I have it on vibrate. It startled me, that's all." The pink scrape mark on her jaw stood out as the rest of her skin paled. She picked up Emma's toy keys and gently cupped the baby's face.

"What's wrong?"

Jake didn't buy the smile she gave him when she looked up to meet his assessing gaze. "I was assaulted last night. What do you expect? Of course I'm jumpy."

"Don't give me that. You found out my name, tracked me down, dolled the kid up—all so you could feed me dinner? I'm not buying it." He reached across the table take hold of the hand she rested there. Jake damned himself for doing it. He damned himself for shifting her grip to hold on. "Something's got you spooked. And whatever you just saw on your phone is part of it."

Setting her phone on top of the table, she showed him the message written there. "My assistant, Mark, keeps texting to tell me this woman I talked to before I left the shop has called three more times asking for me."

"What woman?"

"I answered the first time because I thought she was a reporter."

"What woman, Robin? What did she say?"

"It was a prank call. She sounded drunk. I'm assuming she read about me in the paper."

"And?" Her long, artistic fingers were like ice to the touch. And Jake couldn't seem to stop from stroking his thumb against the pulse in her wrist, trying to instill some warmth into her.

"She said I didn't deserve her." She was holding on with both hands now. "She said I should have died last night."

Jake concentrated every nerve on his grip to keep the surge of anger from fisting his hand too tightly around hers. "Lousy coward. You don't believe that, do you?"

"I don't care what anyone says about me. But she was so adamant about how terrible a mother I am. I know I'm a single mom, but I do my best. I get tired sometimes, but I can support Emma on my own. She has a good doctor, a safe home…" A deep breath shuddered through her. "I read every book, I took classes—so I'd be ready when my chance to have a child came. I fought so hard to have a baby on my own. I don't have that many years left when I can have a healthy pregnancy. But none of the relationships I'd been in were right for starting a family. And none of the science I tried took." She pulled one hand from his and reached over to touch Emma's cheek. "And then this little miracle fell into my lap. I wanted to adopt her as soon as I met her. It was love at first sight."

Even a blind man could see how much Robin adored her daughter and what a fiercely protective mother she was. "This crackpot said you didn't deserve her? I'm assuming she didn't give her name?"

She shook her head. Her gray-blue eyes darkened like a starless night. Her fingers convulsed around his and Jake tightened his grip. "She said I put Emma in harm's way last night."

The bastard who'd attacked Robin had put the baby in harm's way. Did the sliced seat belt and tipped car seat mean that lowlife had been after Emma? Was the attack on Robin collateral damage to the unthinkable crime of kidnapping or hurting her infant daughter? Without thinking, Jake stretched his arm out to touch Emma. But at the last moment, he wised up and settled for returning the slobbery plastic keys to her surprisingly strong grasp. No sense completing a circle that had nothing to do with him—that shouldn't be his concern.

He let go of Robin, too. These weren't his women to protect. He couldn't be swayed by searching eyes and needy grasps. Curling both hands into fists, Jake tried to think like the tough guys on the IDs in his apartment. He had to think like that ruthless survivalist from his nightmares. "You didn't recognize the phone number?"

Robin rubbed her hands together on top of the table, perhaps missing his touch, more likely just feeling chilled again. "She's only called the shop. I don't have caller ID there. She didn't tell me who she was, of course."

"How specific was the threat? Did she mention Emma's name?" So his tone was a little sharper than he intended. That was the whole idea of being a tough guy, right?

"No. But how does she know I'm not her real mother?

Adoptions aren't public record, and only my attorney and friends know I didn't give birth to her. She talked to me like I'd done something wrong, like…like I'm the one who put Emma in danger. She sounded like she wanted to take Emma away from me." He realized that Robin's suspicions were following his own. "KCPD is focusing on the Rose Red Rapist. I'm trying to figure out who's doctoring the books at my shop and stealing from me. Maybe there's someone else out there none of us have thought of whom I need to be worried about."

"Why are you telling me?" Ah, hell. There it was— the trust in those pretty eyes. She was looking at him as though he was the go-to man who could save the day for her. He'd lost enough sleep already fighting that whole damsel in distress complex that could do nothing but get him into trouble. "I don't do relationships, Robin. Of any kind. Don't bring your troubles to me."

"*You're* the one who asked. All I did was offer you dinner." At last, a hint of color dotted her cheeks. Temper. Good. He could deal with anger a lot easier than he could deal with need and trust and trying to be this woman's hero.

"My mistake." Jake slid out of the booth and stood up. "Montgomery!" he shouted at the detective, startling Emma. The little girl dropped her keys and burst into tears. Robin quickly unhooked the baby and lifted her into her arms, cooing comforting words and staring daggers at Jake as the detective looked up from his phone.

"Making friends, Lonergan?" the detective asked.

Wiseass. Jake ignored the knot of guilt that twisted in his stomach at making Emma cry. "Did you find out who owned the car I saw last night?"

"Rental company. It'll require a little more digging to get the driver's name."

Good. KCPD needed to be working this case. Not him.

"Ms. Carter has been getting harassing calls she needs to report." Jake looked back at Robin, absorbing the disappointment that darkened her gaze. "You stay out of my life, lady. Don't come to me again."

"COME ON, SWEETIE." ROBIN DIDN'T know whether to feel anger or humiliation. Something was pulsing through every muscle as she pushed the stroller out the Shamrock Bar's front door. "Did that big, scary man make you cry?"

Robin adjusted the top of the stroller to shade Emma from the late-afternoon sun, and set off at a brisk walk. It had taken a good ten minutes to get Emma calmed down. Singing a soft lullaby, Robin had carried her back and forth through the tables at the Shamrock, while Jake disappeared into the back rooms. She'd reported the disturbing phone call to Detective Montgomery, then gathered her things and strapped Emma into her stroller as the first of the bar's early customers wandered in.

Had she really asked so much of Jake Lonergan? Was it beyond him to give a rat's ass about anyone besides himself?

One minute, he'd been transformed by Emma's curious touches and squeals of delight. The next, he'd been loud and crude and pushing them away as fast as he could. His words said he wanted nothing to do with Robin, yet his touch—rough like a cat's tongue and just as gentle—against her hands and wrist had told a different story. He'd offered comfort and strength, and had hinted at the inexplicable attraction smoldering between them. But he didn't want dinner. He didn't want a thank-you. He didn't want to help and he didn't want her. The man was completely infuriating and Robin had been a first-class fool to think he wanted to get any further involved with her problems.

A car slowed down on the street and drifted toward the curb. Instinctively, Robin steered Emma closer to the brick and concrete block buildings and kept walking.

"You can't have it both ways, Lonergan," she muttered. "Either you're our friend or you're—"

The car's passenger-side window went down, and she realized the car had been keeping pace with her. "Ms. Carter?"

Huh? She jerked to a halt and glanced over at the driver—a man in his mid to late thirties. No one she knew. She took note that the car was black, not green, before shaking off the discomfiture of a stranger calling her by name and starting on her way again.

But her reaction had been confirmation enough for the man to park his car and call out to her again. "It *is* you."

For a brief second, she imagined a black stocking mask, a leering glare and a baseball bat. But the driver wore a suit and tie. The skies were sunny and clear, her vision was good and her imagination was simply working overtime. She couldn't afford to be spooked every time a man spoke to her. She shook her head and urged the stroller forward again. "I don't know you."

He ignored the dismissal and got out of the car. "We're practically family."

Other than a slight stutter in her step, Robin kept walking. Her parents had retired to Arizona and she was an only child. The only family she had in Kansas City was right here in this stroller.

The man buttoned his suit jacket and followed her onto the sidewalk, falling into step a few paces behind her. "Ms. Carter, you're going to have to talk to me. Either here or in a courtroom."

That stopped her. "A courtroom?" Keeping Emma and the stroller behind her, she turned to face him. Maybe six feet tall. Brown hair, green eyes, clean-shaven. Black suit and white shirt like an executive or an attorney would wear. She knew the type. But she didn't know him. "I'm afraid you have me at a disadvantage, Mr....?"

"Houseman. William Houseman. My friends call me Bill."

"Are you a reporter, Mr. Houseman?"

"No." He reached inside his suit jacket and handed her a business card. Robin was half afraid to take it at first, but she supposed a man who meant her harm wouldn't so readily identify himself.

She verified his name on the card. "A banker?"

"What I do for a living isn't important. I just want you to have my contact information."

This one-way familiarity was getting on her nerves. Robin folded the card in her fist. "How do you know me? And don't give me that family story again. We've never met."

Bill Houseman leaned to one side and smiled down at Emma. When he wiggled his finger in Emma's direction and elicited a chortle, Robin pulled the stroller closer to her body. "Actually, your daughter and I are family."

A chill shivered down Robin's spine despite the sun shining down on her. Was this another threat? "*I'm* her family. We have to go."

"I need only a few minutes of your time."

Traffic was picking up as employees in the nearby office buildings got off work. Robin hurried to catch up with a group leaving the business in front of her, but Houseman grabbed her arm. Robin shrugged him off. The people ahead were quickly disappearing into a parking garage. She wasn't going to catch them and Bill Houseman apparently wasn't going to leave her alone.

"Ms. Carter, you and your daughter are in great danger."

The matter-of-fact statement stopped her in her tracks. "Is that a threat?"

"Why? Do you feel threatened?"

With a strange man following her? She took off again. "What do you think? Do you know something about what happened to me last night?"

"I think you'll want to have this conversation in private." He didn't slur his words or ramble the way the woman on the phone had. Yet the effect was the same. This man was a stranger—and he knew a lot more about her than any stranger should.

She'd already passed a couple of buildings, but the intersection up ahead and her shop half a block beyond that seemed miles away. What would be her closest escape route? Going on to her shop? Back to the bar? Straight out into the middle of traffic where he couldn't follow? With no promising option in sight, Robin spun around, trying a more confrontational tactic to get rid of the man strolling behind her. "Did you read about me in the paper? How did you find me?"

"I knew you long before you made the headlines, Ms. Carter." He called her bluff, smiling as he walked past her. But he stopped and turned in front of the stroller. "That's a beautiful baby. What did you name her?"

When he knelt in front of Emma, Robin jerked the stroller back. "Get away from her."

He smiled and rose to his feet. "I think she looks like a Hailey."

"What did you say?" The blood drained from Robin's body, leaving her ice cold. That was Emma's birth name—before the adoption. He *did* know her daughter. This wasn't supposed to happen. "She isn't Hailey anymore. She's *my* daughter. If you want to talk to me, call my attorney and make an appointment."

With fear flagging every step, Robin pushed the stroller around him.

He grabbed her arm as she hurried past, tightening his grip when she tried to shake him off. "This can't wait. I have a favor to ask."

"Let go. If you're who I think you are, you're not supposed to have any contact with me. I'll call the police. I know a detective back in the Shamrock Bar. He's there right now."

"Do you really think you ought to be taking your daughter into a bar?" She could smell the cigarette smoke on his breath as he whispered against her ear. "What kind of mother does that? Do you really have this child's best interests—?"

"The lady said to let her go." Jake Lonergan's deep, menacing voice filled the air, washing over Robin like a protective hug and silencing the accusation in Bill Houseman's voice.

Houseman's grip tightened before he released her and stepped back. "I have business with Ms. Carter."

"Not today, you don't."

Robin wasted no time asking why Jake was here. She quickly pulled Emma back and stood beside him.

Houseman straightened his cuffs beneath his suit jacket. Betraying either nerves or a sudden fastidiousness about his appearance, he adjusted his tie and collar, too. "One way or another, we will have this conversation. Preferably without your Neanderthal friend here. It's important. A matter of life or death, I'm afraid."

"Whose? My baby's?"

Jake shifted at the possible threat, standing tall and immovable, his strong arms crossed over his chest. He'd shed the green apron he'd had on in the bar and looked like some sort of human tank blocking the sidewalk. He'd come to Robin's rescue. Again.

"No. But it's important. In a way, I'm trying to save you, too."

"From what?"

Houseman seemed to consider continuing the conversation for about three seconds. His gaze skipped over Jake and he looked at Robin. "Please give me a call."

With a subtle shift in his stance, Jake was suddenly positioned between her and Houseman. He'd even barred Emma from the man's direct line of sight. Although there seemed to be more that Houseman wanted to say, the man clearly didn't want to push his luck with Jake there. After a nod to Robin and a 'Bye, little one' to Emma, he returned to his car, started the engine and drove away.

"Thank you." Robin flattened her palm against Jake's back and felt him shiver at the unexpected touch. He moved away far too quickly to think she'd done anything more than startle him. Swallowing her pride, she let him put the distance between them that he apparently needed. "I didn't handle that very well. I couldn't think. I panicked. I guess I'm still rattled from last night."

"Is the kid okay?"

"Yes. He touched her, but he didn't hurt her." Robin stooped down to check on Emma. Straps, secure. Blanket, fine. Blue eyes smiling and content. "I guess he didn't do anything except…give me his business card." She wound her fingers around the edge of the stroller as the strength ebbed from her. "I know this name. I didn't know him, but the last name…I've seen it in legal documents." She let Emma capture her finger in a tiny fist. "He said he was family."

"What are you talking about?"

"Houseman. Emma's birth mother—I never met her but…her last name is Houseman." She held up the crumpled card for Jake to read. "Like him. Is he Emma's father? Does he want her back? I can't lose her."

Jake didn't take the card or speculate an answer to her question. Instead, he cupped his hand beneath Robin's elbow and pulled her to her feet. If she thought he was being polite or showing concern, she was mistaken. He positioned her behind the stroller and gave it a nudge, forcing her to grab on to the handle and get moving before he pushed Emma down the sidewalk without her. "Like I said before—tell the cops about that phone call. This guy, too. And quit wandering off on your own. I won't always be here to save you."

Gratitude and irritation warred inside her. "Then why did you? If I'm such a burden, if we're such an intrusion on your life, why did you come all the way down the block and get rid of Mr. Houseman for me?"

"It's my job to keep trouble away from the bar."

"Like men who accost women on the street?"

"Like you, lady." He scanned the sidewalk and street as they walked, and Robin realized that she, too, was learning to check inside every car and doorway for anyone who might be watching or waiting for them as they walked past. "I'll take you to the corner, and watch you down to your shop. But then you are no longer my responsibility, understand? We're done."

Again.

Chapter Seven

"What are you doing in here, boss lady?"

Startled by the interruption, Robin crumpled the sick note she'd been rereading and stuffed it into the pocket of her apron. She looked up from the stool where she sat in the shop's refrigerated stockroom to see Mark Riggins standing in the open doorway.

I'm taking your baby.

Mark was unrolling the sleeves of his shirt and buttoning the cuffs at the wrist. "It's quittin' time."

Gathering her wits and taking note of the late hour, Robin set the last handful of gerbera daisies she'd been counting back into their vase on the bottom shelf and entered the number on her clipboard before getting up.

She pulled her sweater more tightly around her neck and hugged her arms at her waist. "Are the boutonnieres for the Vanderham second wedding finished?"

"Packaged and ready for delivery in the morning. Along with two dozen small sprays and the biggest altar piece I've ever put together. Tacky and too much, but if it makes the client happy, who am I to complain?" Frowning, he took a step into the cold room. "Are you okay? You look a little pale. Are you thinking about the assault again?"

Was there a moment in the week since her attack that she hadn't? She slipped her hand into her apron pocket, feeling today's latest threat burning against her fingers. But her personal problems weren't Mark's concern—or anyone else's, apparently, according to the police's inability to act on a few prank calls and messages. So she pasted on a reassuring smile. "No. I didn't realize it was nine o'clock. Is everything locked up?"

"You bet." Mark inclined his head toward the workrooms in the back. "We're all getting ready to head out so we can get an early start on tomorrow's setup. I think Linda and Christine are going out for coffee, but the rest of us are heading home. You should do the same."

"I know." Since the assault nearly a week earlier, she'd taken every safety precaution she knew to heart—especially since that first drunken phone call had turned into some sort of anonymous hate mail campaign. Every day there'd been something new in her bills and correspondence at the shop. And each letter, sent from a Kansas City post office with no return address, had grown more disturbing by the day.

The Rose Red Rapist didn't make mistakes and would come back to finish what he'd started.

A single woman had no business adopting a child.

Emma would be taken from her and Robin would be punished for abandoning her the night of the attack.

Abandon? As if she'd been given a choice.

At one point she'd considered digging out Bill Houseman's card and calling him to find out if he was behind the terror campaign. He'd claimed to be related to Emma, and this could be his sick effort to get her to reverse the adoption so he could take custody of the baby. But how could the attempted rape be related to a legal claim? Besides, a call to Robin's attorney had assured her that the adoption was legitimate and airtight, and there was nothing requiring her to have any contact with the birth parents who'd surrendered their rights to Emma.

The motive might not be clear, but the message was unmistakable. Some nut job had fixated on Robin and Emma, and it was up to her to maintain a vigilance that would keep her, and everyone around her, safe.

She pulled herself from her thoughts and smiled her thanks to Mark. "Will you make sure that no one leaves by themselves?"

"Sure. I'll ask Leon to move the van and secure the loading dock, too."

"Thanks." Even though she'd be making the rounds herself to make sure everything was locked up tight before she left, it was reassuring to have a second pair of eyes checking the security of the place. "I need a few minutes to get things back in order here and pack up Emma. Then we'll be leaving, too."

Mark let the door close behind him and joined her in the middle of the tall, metal shelves that lined the room. "What are you doing?"

She exhaled a weary sigh that clouded around her face. "Old-fashioned inventory, counting out the flowers we have in stock one at a time."

"Sounds tedious. Want some help?"

Robin smiled and shook her head. "It's nearly done. Besides, you've been talking about those late dinner plans of yours all day long. You need to skedaddle."

"My date can wait," he volunteered.

She waved off the offer and picked up one of the long, narrow boxes she'd set on the floor. "At first I thought maybe a couple of orders hadn't been logged in. But then you showed me your records and I realized we were just encoding entries differently." She laid the box on a matching stack and opened the lid. "Now I'm thinking the number error is coming from the distributor's end. We were shorted two stems in each of these boxes. If that's been going on the entire time I was gone, that adds up to over two thousand dollars."

"I'll call them and ask what's going on. Get them to adjust the billing." Mark thumbed over his shoulder. "In the meantime, if you won't be too much longer, I promised Shirley I'd walk her to her car."

"You go ahead. I just need to push this pallet out of the main path and shut off the lights in here." She turned the handle of the pallet mover and released the brake. "I'll be out shortly."

"Good." He pulled the handle on the insulated steel door and pushed it open. "Shirley, my love, are you ready for your escort?"

Robin smiled at his over-the-top charm. She was glad she and Mark had sat down together to work out the book-keeping issues. It was a relief to finally feel like she'd gotten back into the routine of work and running her shop. Heaven knew that, except for Emma's bright shining star, her personal life was still a complicated mess.

Inhaling a resolute breath and refusing to let the fear those letters and phone calls engendered take hold of her again, Robin leaned her shoulder into the pallet mover to start it rolling. By the time she'd parked it out of the way and retrieved her clipboard, she was back in cool, calm and collected mode. She went to the door and pushed.

But nothing happened.

She quickly squelched that bubble of fear that had never truly left her and pushed the handle again.

Nothing.

She jiggled the handle one more time and pressed the emergency release latch. Only, something had jammed and it wouldn't engage the lock. This door wasn't opening. At least, not from her side.

"Mark?" She knocked on the door to see if anyone was on the other side. "Shirley? Leon?" Robin knocked again. "Hello? I'm in here."

Someone had gotten a little overzealous with the locking-up directive. At least she hoped it was an accident—that whoever had slipped the locking pin into the other side of the door handle simply hadn't realized she was in here, and that, considering recent events, this wasn't some poorly timed joke.

"Hello?"

The same insulated walls that kept her from hearing anything outside the fridge room were probably muffling her shouts, as well. Maybe the guys were walking the female employees to their cars and no one was out there. It was impossible to hear through the thick door unless they were standing in the adjoining hallway.

A fearful suspicion simmered inside her. But she tamped down the panic and tried to think this through. Had she stayed in here longer than she thought? She reached for her cell phone, but that was in the diaper bag in her office. She found the tiny canister of pepper spray in the pocket of her jeans. She'd started carrying it again after that awful night. But she was locked in, not under attack. At least it was a walk-in refrigerator, not a freezer. Things could get mighty uncomfortable, but she wouldn't die in here. And this door wasn't the only way out.

"Ugh. Robin." She chided the foreboding that had momentarily silenced logic and ran over to check the delivery entrance where they loaded and unloaded large orders through the double doors. She rattled the handle on one, tried them both. But nothing budged. Normally, this was padlocked from the outside unless they were using it. "Leon?" Maybe he was back there with the van. She flattened her palm against the cold steel and pounded. "Leon!"

Everything was locked up tight. Just the way she wanted it. Two sets of locked doors to keep anyone from sneaking into the shop from the back alley.

Two sets of locked doors that trapped her in between.

The panic bubbled over and Robin ran back to the hallway door and pounded again. "Hey! Mark? Anyone? I'm locked in!"

Robin was trapped. But that wasn't what scared her.

She couldn't get to Emma, who was sleeping peacefully in Robin's office. Unguarded. Alone.

This was no accident. And it was certainly no joke.

I'm taking your daughter.

Forget cool, calm and collected. Robin pounded on the door and shouted. "Help! Let me out!"

JAKE LEANED AGAINST the top railing of the fence surrounding the Fairy Tale Bridal parking lot and watched the lights in Robin's shop go out one by one. Careful not to let the glare from the street lamp reflect off the face of his watch and alert anyone to his presence, he checked the time. 9:00 p.m. sharp. Good. He appreciated punctuality when it came to security.

Robin Carter had been consistent for four nights in a row now. He'd seen her lock the front door, check the windows, turn out the lights and walk to the parking lot with the rest of her staff before loading that bulky baby carrier into the backseat and driving off to whatever all-American suburban home they lived in.

Despite his best intentions to forget the leggy brunette and her blue-eyed baby, despite every lick of sense that said he shouldn't care about her troubles or get involved any further in their lives, Jake had planned his dinner break from the bar just before nine. And for the past four nights, he'd made the brisk walk around the corner to this hiding place away from the bridal shop's security cameras, and watched to make sure the Carter girls got safely out of this neighborhood where too many innocent women had gotten hurt.

He justified his sneaky voyeurism as a matter of mental survival. He refused to care about Robin and Emma on any personal level, but a man had to live with his conscience. Jake had enough violence and unanswered questions haunting his dreams. He didn't need his waking moments to be plagued with doubts and guilt, too. He could watch from a distance without interacting with them, and appease his conscience by making sure they were safe without risking developing any personal connection to them.

Knowing his black shirt and dark jeans helped him blend in with the ivy vines trailing over the fence, he rolled his neck and allowed himself to stretch out some of the kinks of fatigue that came from standing in one position for so long. At least this was an easier gig than that night he'd spent out in the rain waiting for Robin to reappear. Not that he minded the elements. He'd needed to see her that night to make sure she was okay—that his own self-preservation instincts hadn't left her exposed to any more danger.

Apparently, he still needed to see her to put his conscience to rest each night. But there wouldn't be any more hand-holding or running his fingers through her hair or thinking about kissing her. There wouldn't be any more stabs of protective jealousy and charging to the rescue when some other man put his hands on her. Despite his ugly facade, he was a man who wanted and lusted and could learn to care, just like any other man. But Jake knew that the monster he might also be made him too dangerous to ever give in to those normal wants and needs. If he knew he was responsible for hurting Robin or her daughter, it would open up a wound no one would ever see, and from which he might never recover.

Jake stilled again to watch the progression across the street. Like clockwork, the back door opened beneath the green-and-white awning and the employees of the Robin's Nest Floral Shop came out.

The dark-haired guy with the bow tie came out with the middle-aged blonde. Good. Bow-tie guy was walking her to her car. They laughed about something before she got in and drove away. Bow-tie guy waited as two more women came out together, got into their cars and drove away.

"Hey!" Hearing the slam of a door, Jake moved his attention back the shop entrance. A young man in a green uniform shirt jogged out and stopped Bow-tie guy outside his car. With his senses going on alert, Jake leaned forward, turning his ear to eavesdrop as their conversation flared into a heated argument.

He was too far away to catch everything, but Jake quickly realized this was not as happy a family of co-workers as he'd expected. Uniform kid said something about "...your fault."

Bow-tie guy kept his cool while the younger man blew up.

"Ms. Carter...twice now."

"...not going to lose your job."

"I'll take care of it if you won't."

Interesting.

Almost as quickly as it had started, the argument stopped. The two men separated to their respective vehicles. Both immediately pulled out their cell phones, either taking or making calls as they got into their cars. The younger man started his car and sped out of the parking lot while the older man sat inside his car, chatting on the phone.

Had Robin made a discovery about the accounting discrepancy she'd been stewing over that night she'd been attacked? Not a smart move to confront Uniform guy on her own. A man wouldn't have to be built like Jake to out-muscle her if he really wanted to.

Jake's blood heated in his veins at the thought of Robin getting hurt again. Three more minutes passed before Bow-tie guy ended his call. He watched the back door for two minutes more before checking the time and then driving away. Jake's feet itched to follow one or both of those men to find out what they'd been arguing about, if it had to do with Robin and what calls were so important that they had to be made before they'd even left the parking lot.

And where the hell was Robin, anyway?

Changing the kid's diaper? Dinking with those books again? The whole idea of safety in numbers was that she had to *be* with those numbers.

Jake checked his watch again. It was a full fifteen minutes after closing and her rental car was the only one left in the lot. "Walk out to your car, Robin," Jake willed, hating the instinct that warned him he needed to get over to that shop now. "Five more minutes," he argued with that darker urge.

Several more cars were parked on the street in front of the shop—maybe one of those belonged to a last-minute customer. The goal of coming here was to make sure she was safe—not to talk to her, touch her or be some kind of hero to her again. That wasn't the role he was here to play tonight.

He bargained with the silent red alert churning through

his blood by slipping out of his hiding place and moving down the street to scan for the green sedan that had been watching her place the other night. There was no green car, but there was plenty of traffic tonight—people leaving work, others pulling into empty spaces to try out the coffee bar or dance club on the corner.

Funny how nobody noticed a man strolling through the shadows if he didn't want to be noticed. A trio of women heading into the club breezed right by him, either too eager to get to the party or too ignorant of the dangers of this neighborhood to pay him any mind. A young couple exited the coffee bar. The woman bumped Jake's shoulder as he turned the corner, and she mumbled an apology without taking her attention away from the man she was with.

Was he really that good at blending in? Or were these covert skills an unfortunate byproduct of having a face that no one really wanted to look at? Pretty good cover for a hit man or whatever kind of lowlife he might have been in his forgotten past.

Swallowing the bile that the possibility of being that kind of man invariably triggered in him, Jake walked another half a block without any sign of the green sedan and turned into the alley behind the businesses to make his way back to Robin's shop. He hoped her car was gone before he had to get back to finish his shift at the Shamrock. And if she was still there...

What the hell?

Jake pulled back against the bricks when he recognized Bow-tie guy from the shop pulling into a parking space and getting out. Maybe the guy had an aversion to exercise and half a block was too far to walk after work. But those sly looks up and down the street before reaching back into the car and pulling out a flat manila envelope made Jake think this stop wasn't about laziness. When

Bow-tie guy walked to the car parked directly in front of him and climbed into the passenger side, Jake's suspicions jumped up another notch.

He inched out of the shadows to read the plate number of the first car and try to get a glimpse of the driver. The angle was wrong to see a face, but the dark clothes and general build could have been a match for the man in the green sedan the night of the assault. Was this a different rental car? If so, why would the guy go to so much trouble to cover his tracks and mask his identity? Or was this the guy who'd accosted Robin outside the Shamrock? Could they be the same man?

What *was* clear were the unmistakable signs of an exchange taking place. Bow-tie guy opened the envelope and pulled out a pair of photographs. Again, the angle was wrong to see the images clearly, but Jake thought he could make out a dark round halo that could be a head of hair. Pictures of Robin? Emma? Something else? The driver quickly pushed the photos down into the seat between them and pulled a business-size envelope from his jacket. He didn't need Bow-tie guy to open the envelope to know that it was cash.

Jake took another step onto the sidewalk, thinking how easy it would be to get into Bow-tie's car and be waiting for him when he returned. He didn't doubt that he could get a few answers out of him. But the driver pulled out a cell phone and Jake saw the gloves he was wearing—on a balmy spring night—and realized that he was the bigger threat.

If this interchange was a threat at all. Jake inhaled a deep, steadying breath as the driver pulled the phone from his ear and asked Bow-tie a question before returning to his call. Had it always been his nature to suspect a conspiracy wherever he looked? What if there was an innocent explanation for this? Bow-tie had printed some pictures for a friend. He'd designed a floral arrangement and been paid a commission for his work. Even if it was something a little less savory, like selling porn or insider trading, it didn't necessarily have anything to do with the danger lurking around Robin and Emma.

Except… Ah, hell. Of all the people in this busy neighborhood to finally notice him, the driver glanced up into his rearview mirror, then turned in his seat to look right at Jake.

Maybe he suspected Jake was a cop who'd seen the questionable transaction. Maybe the driver just wanted to know why he was curious about his business.

Either way, the meeting was done. The man with the gloves ended the call. Bow-tie guy scrambled out of the car. The driver pulled out and turned the corner, heading north toward Robin's shop. Jake obeyed his instincts, even if he didn't understand where they came from. Ducking back into the alley, he ran its length until he burst out into the parking lot, just in time to see a dark-clothed figure scurrying across the sidewalk and jumping into a car parked in front of the shop.

Had he been *in* the shop? With Robin?

"Hey!" Jake shouted.

Just as the car squealed out of its parking space, the rental car he'd been watching jerked to a stop behind it and honked. The near collision didn't worry Jake as much as the bad timing.

Breathing hard at the unexpected race he'd run, Jake swore and took off across the parking lot. Robin's car was still here. And there was no mistaking it was hers because of the car seat strapped into the back. "Fool woman."

He ran straight to the sidewalk when the car slowed down, making sure the driver could see him there waiting for him in case he was thinking about stopping. Damn those instincts. The car had slowed, but when Jake ran a few yards farther, the brake lights flashed and it jerked to a stop. Jake hustled his legs to catch up to get a good look in the window at the man he suspected was harassing Robin. But when he reached the glass and closed his hand around the door handle, all he saw was a camera flash. "Son of a…"

Blinded for a split second, he could do little more than spin away as the driver gunned the engine. It sped through the yellow light at the next intersection to the screeching protest of car horns and disappeared into the night. Right. Nothing suspicious about that.

"Robin." Jake's chest heaved in and out as he muttered her name, unsure whether he was voicing a hope or cursing himself for what he was about to do.

"Robin!" He dashed past the empty car in the parking lot and banged on the steel exit door. But one knock and the door bounced against his fist.

Unlocked.

Not a good sign. Every cell in his body screamed that something was wrong here. Every instinct told him Robin was in trouble.

Reaching down, he pulled the hunting knife from his boot. Then he took a silent, steadying breath, fisted his hand around the door handle and swung it open.

He slid inside to the glow of security lights and flattened his back against the brick wall beside the door, allowing himself a few seconds to acclimate to the eerie shadows. The only hint that anyone was still here was the sliver of light peeking out beneath the closed door of Robin's office at the end of the hall.

Jake's blood simmered in his veins. Working late with the back door wide open? A scan through the workrooms revealed the back of the shop was empty and that nothing seemed out of place. Maybe she wasn't working at all. Maybe her attacker had come back to finish what he'd started. Maybe that Houseman guy outside the Shamrock was here to finish that conversation that had upset her so. Maybe the threat in the phone call she'd tried to tell him about had become a reality and she was lying in that office injured, unconscious again, or worse. How many times did this woman have to be hurt before she wised up and put her safety before her job? How many times did he have to come bail her out?

If stealth wasn't vital to securing the place, Jake would be cursing up a blue streak. He was as ticked off about Robin putting herself in a position to get hurt as he was the fact that it made him sick to think she might have gotten hurt. Preparing for the worst-case scenario, Jake pressed his back against the hallway wall and crept through the darkness toward that light. He could just bet, too, that she was here alone, that she hadn't told anyone she was working late. Maybe she was counting on Bow-tie guy to walk her to her car. She'd put her trust in some traitorous schlub who wasn't coming back....

That's when he heard the muffled shouts. Punctuated by a thumping that vibrated through the wall at his back, he pinpointed the source of the muted cries for help. They weren't coming from her office. They were close by. Was there another locked room in here? A closet?

He flipped around to the opposite wall to use his eyes to search.

"Stay away from her." Thump. Thump. Thump.

Robin? He zeroed in on the source of the sound and found the seams of a door, camouflaged to match the wallpaper around it.

And then he saw the steel pin wedged into the door

handle. A walk-in refrigerator, like the one at the bar. The chain that hung from the pin rattled with every thump. She'd been locked inside.

He removed the pin and yanked the door open. "Rob—"

"Stay the hell away from my baby!"

Jake dodged a blast of pepper spray, catching Robin by the wrist and knocking the canister from her grip. But not before the stinging chemical splashed his neck.

"Jake? I'm sorry. I thought…" She froze for a second, her wrist pinned to the wall beneath his hand, her eyes glued to the knife he still held, her face blanched with shock and confusion.

"Ah, hell." He tucked the blade into his belt and released her. "Don't you have any sense, lady? You know what I thought?"

Instead of answering, she shoved him back a step. "Emma!"

She charged down the hall and Jake ran after. "I haven't secured that end of the building yet." He grabbed her by the arm, but she twisted away and shot through her office door. "Damn it!"

He caught the door before it slammed back in his face and followed her into the room. "I just disarmed you. How are you going to defend yourself now? You're running blind into an unknown situation. Your outside door is swinging wide open. Nobody else is here. There's nothing good about this scenario. You want to tell me what the hell is going on?"

Completely ignoring every stern warning, she hurried across the room to Emma's bassinet.

"Robin—"

"Shh." Seriously? She pressed a finger to her lips before leaning over the white basket. Then she reached inside and whispered a prayer.

Ignoring the burning skin at his collar and his fuming frustration, Jake toned it down a notch as she pulled up the cover. He sure as hell didn't want to be responsible for scaring Emma again. "Is the kid okay?"

"Sleeping." She smiled as tears spilled over her cheeks. "Like a baby."

And then she crossed the room and walked into him. No, she burrowed into Jake's chest. She pressed her cheek against his pounding heart and wrapped her arms around his waist, clinging to him the way a drowning woman clung to a life preserver. "Thank you." She hiccuped a sound and squeezed him a little tighter. "Thank you."

The emotions that had raged through Jake's system—concern, anger, suspicion—short-circuited.

"Ah, hell. Robin?" Forgetting that this was all kinds of dangerous, Jake wound an arm behind her waist and palmed the back of her head, holding on just as tight. She quivered against him before settling impossibly closer, nestling her head beneath his chin, imprinting his body with the memory of small, sweet breasts, long thighs and firm hips. Was she crying? Shaking with anger? He'd been chasing a suspicious employee and a mystery player with a lot of money and a collection of photographs. What had she been dealing with in here? "I'm sorry. I shouldn't have yelled."

"No, you shouldn't have. You scared the tar out of me with that giant knife. And I was already…" She fisted her hand and pressed it against his shoulder, a friendly reprimand rather than a punch. Good. He was glad she still had the gumption to call him on his crude lack of manners. Made him feel a little less like the bad guy here. But then her fist opened up and her fingers dug into his shirt in one of those clutching grasps that made him crazy, and the skin and muscle underneath danced in response to the needy contact. She was burrowing in again and Jake couldn't seem to remember why this was a bad idea.

"Already what?" He tunneled his fingers beneath her hair to find chilled skin at her nape. Oh, man. How long had she been locked up in there? His shoulders seemed to shift of their own volition, folding around her to surround her in warmth. He'd rethink this whole embrace thing tomorrow. Right now he felt like he needed to hold on to her, too. Like touching her was the only way he could convince those worrisome instincts of his that she was all right. Just like she'd needed to see and touch her baby to know that Emma was safe. Only, Robin wasn't all right. She was shivering. "Honey, you've got to talk to me. I can't keep coming over here to watch you every damn night and keep tabs on all the idiots who work for you—"

"You've been watching…? Did you just call me *honey?*"

"Sorry. I didn't mean—"

"I was kind of hoping you did mean it." With a heavy sigh that moved against him like a caress, Robin released her death grip and took a step back. "You sure you want to call me that, though? You keep showing up to save me and I bring the police into your life—which clearly makes you uncomfortable—and then I…hurt you." She gently touched the irritation mark the pepper spray had left on his skin. The faint sheen of tears that sparkled in her eyes at the damage she'd done to him was more apology than he needed.

He pulled her hand away and clasped it between them. "It's not like I haven't been hurt before. And by a lot bigger and meaner than you, I'm guessin.'"

"You guess?" She reached up and cupped the side of his jaw, gently tracing the scar there with the pad of her thumb. "You don't know who did this to you? Oh, Jake." Lifting her other hand, she brushed her fingers across the rigid scar that bisected his temple. "That bastard should be drawn and quartered for hurting you like this. I can't imagine how much pain you must have suffered. Is that why you don't like Detective Montgomery? Because the police didn't find your attacker?"

She was talking unsolved crime, extending that protective maternal shield to include him in her fierce compassion. But the stroke of her fingers across his skin was eliciting something far more sensual than anything he'd feel for somebody's mother. And he hadn't been thinking about the clue he'd inadvertently revealed about his blank slate of a life. He hadn't been thinking, period.

"Robin," he prompted, trying to convince them both that that endearment and any mention of his past had been slips of the tongue and nothing more. His body was still warm, his concentration still misfiring, after holding her. He didn't need her to keep putting her hands on him, touching him the way a pretty woman touched a normal man. If he was smart, he'd put some distance between them. Jake pulled her hands from his hair and face and retreated to the door, ostensibly checking to make sure no one else was in the building. "What's going on? You didn't get locked in by accident, did you?"

"I don't think so." She swiped the tears from her face and picked up a bulky, plain white business envelope. "I mean, at first, I thought my staff had forgotten I was still here. But I got this in the mail today. There was no message like the others."

"Others?"

Robin handed him the envelope and backed away as though its touch repulsed her. Then she nodded toward the stack of papers on the corner of her desk. "I've gotten something every day, ever since that article about my attack was in the paper. Phone calls, too. I reported them to Detective Montgomery. But he said until the creep actually does something, there's not much KCPD can do."

"Do you think Houseman is behind this?"

"I don't know. He calls me every day, saying it's urgent we talk, but it has to be in person. At least he identifies himself. I keep putting him off."

She hugged her arms around her waist as Jake picked up one letter and unfolded it. "Son of a…"

It was a photocopy of Robin, a blurry image taken of her pushing Emma in her stroller on the sidewalk outside the shop. Robin's face had been x'ed out with a marker and a cryptic message had been scribbled across the bottom. *You don't deserve her.*

"Are they all like this?"

"Variations on the same theme. I'm an unfit mother. I deserved what happened to me. He's coming to take my baby away." Her gaze fixated on the envelope Jake still held. "There aren't any words in that one, but I get the message loud and clear. He can get to us. He *has* gotten to us."

He opened the envelope to find shredded bits of soiled yellow yarn inside. The frayed strands were of the narrowest skein— The remnants of a baby's knit cap? "Is this Emma's?"

The tiny cap hadn't just unraveled and gotten dirty. Someone had taken scissors or a knife to it. Someone who'd been very, very angry. "She was wearing it the night of the attack. I wondered why I couldn't find it afterward. He must have taken it as a souvenir. I thought an attempted rape was frightening enough, but this…this scares me." She moved back to the bassinet to watch her daughter sleep. "I thought he'd locked me in the fridge room tonight so that he could kidnap her. I don't know how he got in. I was running late, but there should have been someone else here, waiting for us in the parking lot." She spun around as a new concern hit her and hurried toward the door. "Are they all right? Did anyone else get hurt?"

Jake grabbed her arm before she could get by him and blocked her exit. Before she could voice a protest, he placed the envelope back in her hand and released her. "They all left."

"They left?"

"Ten minutes after closing, your parking lot was empty."

"You *were* watching. But…" She seemed to be having a tough time processing that she'd been abandoned by her employees. Shaking her head, she returned the envelope with Emma's cap to her desk. "It must have been a miscommunication. Mark thought Leon was waiting for us—Leon thought Mark was."

"One of them could have locked you in and then driven away."

"I refuse to believe that." Would she refuse to believe her employee was selling pictures that could have been of her or Emma? "Everyone here cares about my daughter. We celebrated her arrival. They all want to take care of her when she's here. They wouldn't put her in danger. What would be their motive for the assault and these threats?"

"You said you suspected someone was cooking the books."

The fire in her eyes was coming back as she got defensive of her people. "Why go to all this trouble to cover up an embezzlement? We're talking about two thousand dollars, not millions."

"I've seen people do worse for less." Had he?

"The people I know don't act that way."

"Then someone you *don't* know waited until he could sneak in unnoticed."

She drifted a step closer. "I thought you were watching."

Jake braced his hands on his hips and squared off against her. "I thought you'd have enough sense to leave with the others."

"If you're going to spy on me, at least do a thorough job."

"You're not my responsibility, lady. I don't owe you anything."

He raised his voice to match the accusation in hers. The baby cooed in her bassinet, stirring in her sleep.

Robin palmed Jake's biceps and nudged him out the door. "Could we take this out in the hallway so we don't wake Emma?" She stepped into the shadows with him, resuming the discussion in a more rational tone as soon as she closed the door. "Are you sure you didn't see anyone come inside?"

She'd come to him for help, and now she was blaming him? "I left for a few minutes to see if I could find the car that was watching you the other night."

"Did you see it?"

Jake scraped his palm over his stubbled jaw, stifling a curse. He *was* to blame. He'd dropped the ball tonight, getting distracted while the real danger was close at hand. "I thought I saw something suspicious, but I can't be sure. There was a car out front pulling away when I ran back. Still couldn't make out the driver. A guy in the car I'd been tailing snapped a picture of me and drove off in a hurry."

"There were two men?"

"Possibly." Maybe her assistant's rendezvous hadn't been about the pictures at all. Maybe it had been a ruse to get him away from the shop so an accomplice could get inside to Robin and Emma. Jake had suspected two people had been involved the night of her assault—the attacker and a getaway driver. Maybe the tag team had been back at work tonight.

"Jake. What are you thinking?"

"That it's a good thing I came back." He pulled the knife from his belt and slipped it back into the sheath inside his boot. "I may have scared off the guy before he could get to Emma. I made a lot of noise running through the alley."

"Why would he want your picture?"

"That was the other guy. He may have been using the flash to blind me."

When Jake pulled his pant leg down over the top of his boot and straightened, he could see she wasn't listening to his explanation. She was staring at the weaponry attached to his leg. "Is that a gun?"

"Yeah."

"Do you know how to use it?"

Too well, perhaps. "Yeah."

She tilted her eyes up to his. "Are you some kind of cop?"

I honestly don't know. "Don't worry. The safety's on. It's not going to accidentally go off around Emma. Or you."

She touched her fingers to the middle of his chest. "That's not what I asked. Why are you carrying a concealed gun?"

"Because I can in Missouri."

She drew in a soft gasp that echoed in the hallway. "That's not an answer."

The security lights were too dim to tell what emotion darkened her eyes, but he could see them darting back and forth. She was trying to figure him out. *Join the crowd, honey.* She was trying to resolve the dangerous man he was with the hero she wanted him to be. Allow him to clarify. He leaned in, pressing his chest against her open palm, backing her into the wall without moving a step. He moved into her personal space and watched her pupils dilate with fear. "Don't mistake me for Prince Charming."

"I dated Prince Charming. It didn't work." Her voice hushed to a throaty whisper. Uh-oh. Backfire. Was she flirting with him? Even worse, was he playing this game with her? Their emotions must be too on edge for him to be thinking straight. "You've been watching the shop every night? Most people would think that's creepy—you, armed and dangerous, spying on me from the shadows."

"I am creepy."

"No, you're not." She brought up her other hand to rest it against his chest. Only, her hands weren't resting. They were moving, smoothing out the wrinkles in his shirt, petting him. "Don't say things like that."

Jake shrugged. She thought that *telling* him to stop being such a wiseass would get him to stop? He could snap her in two like a toothpick if he wanted to. Yet she somehow saw past the attitude and the ugliness, and never once backed down from arguing with him. Either she was a fool, or he was. And he was beginning to think it was the latter. "I've been coming over on my dinner break. You made me feel guilty that day at the bar."

"That wasn't my intention."

"Wasn't it? Didn't you want me to get involved?" Jake flattened his hands on the wall on either side of her head and leaned in another fraction of an inch. He was making one last try at intimidating her out of this hero-worship thing that toyed so recklessly with the emotions he normally kept in check. But he breathed in her flowery, feminine scent and knew he was toast. His whole body buzzed with anticipation and he hadn't even touched her.

"Yes. If you were involved… I'm used to handling

whatever life throws at me on my own, Jake. Business issues. Personal disappointments. Family responsibilities. But I can't handle this. If you would help…" She swallowed her nerves and Jake watched the movement all the way down her creamy throat. Her eyes were dark like the twilight sky when she tilted them up to his. "I need you. You're the biggest, baddest S.O.B. I know. I don't think that creep will keep messing with us if you're around."

Jake nodded. He liked that answer. It was honest. Probably true. He was all kinds of wrong for this woman. But he liked the way she talked. He liked the way her pale skin glowed in the hazy light. He liked the fresh, pure female scent of her filling his head. And he liked the way she touched him, putting her hands on him like she wasn't afraid to.

A better man would have pushed away from the wall and let the night air cool the heat between them. But Jake wasn't that man. Instead of walking away, instead of doing the polite thing and retreating a step, he closed the distance between their lips and kissed her. He curled his fingers into the burlap weave of the wall behind her, bracing himself for a shove in the chest. The kiss was as gentle as he knew how to make it, and that wasn't very. He was hungry to taste what kind of woman she was. All lady? All fire? Some combination of both? He pressed his mouth down on hers, tilting her head back. He sucked her bottom lip between his and stroked his tongue along its cool softness until it warmed and quivered and parted from its mate, releasing a tender sigh across his grizzled cheek.

Confused by her lack of resistance, Jake pulled back, his eyes seeking hers in the shadows. He didn't realize he'd asked a question, but Robin nodded. "Like this." Then she tugged on his chin to align his mouth more fully with hers, and stretched up to seal their lips in a decadent, openmouthed kiss.

Branded by an unexpected rush of heat, Jake threaded his fingers into her hair and cupped her head to hold her against the driving force of his desire. Her back hit the wall and his body followed as he plunged his tongue into her mouth, plundering her lips, drinking in her heat and tasting her welcome. He knew how badly he wanted Robin, but he hadn't known how much he needed her to want him a little bit, too. Not just as some kind of monster to scare away the bad guys, but as a man.

That she'd taken charge of the kiss, that she framed his jaw and pulled him to her, that her lips and tongue were inviting him to do the same sweet things to her she was doing to him, was as heady and healing and normal as anything he'd felt since losing himself to that bullet.

Her mouth was soft and warm and delicious as he claimed it again and again. Her hair was silky and strong tangled between his fingers. Her soft, throaty moans skittered over him like a physical touch, eliciting a husky groan of his own. Her fingertips bit into his chest, his shoulders, then skimmed up the column of his neck to hold on to his battered face again.

Jake needed, and he took. Robin gave and he humbly thanked her. She was sweet and sexy and everything he could ever want. The kiss was raw and passionate and maybe just a little bit rough. They were linked by hands and lips and the fiery heat igniting between them. But Jake felt a connection being forged deep inside him, a bond to this woman that felt more real and right than any hazy memory of the life he'd lived.

And because of that connection, because it was already too late for a man who didn't want to get involved to deny his feelings for this woman, Jake ended the kiss. He was too weak to completely break away, though, so he rested his forehead against hers. Robin was breathing as hard as he was, but she stood tall and strong with him. Her hands settled at the base of his throat, providing an unexpected cooling balm to the injured skin there. He eased his grip in her hair and opened his eyes to find her looking right up at him. Her cheeks were flushed with heat and the pink abrasion his beard had left around her mouth looked as if he'd stamped himself there. He'd expected her to look as dazed as he felt.

But there was a purpose in those gray-blue eyes, a directness that seemed to indicate she felt that same connection, too. She was asking the silent question now and Jake nodded. "He won't mess with you," he vowed. "Or Emma. I'm involved."

Maybe he'd just been expertly played. Flirt with the big monster. Give him some sugar. Get his heart and hormones racing so hard that he'd do anything to get another kiss, some tender touches and maybe something more—all in exchange for getting involved in Robin Carter's problems and making them go away.

Didn't matter if he'd been played or not. And he might well regret it. But he wasn't going anywhere now. There were too many strange things happening around this tiny family. He intended to keep them both safe. Or die trying.

At last Jake found the strength to pull his hands from her mussed hair and back some distance between them. "Pack your things. I'll call Robbie and tell him I won't be back tonight. I'll need to make a stop by my place. Then I'm taking you home."

Chapter Eight

"I love what you've done with the place."

Robin set Emma's carrier on the small, laminate-topped counter that passed for a kitchen in Jake's tiny apartment. Other than the weightlifting equipment in one corner, Jake's apartment looked as old and out of date as the dingy limestone facade outside.

"All the comforts of home," his tone mocked, "if *comfortable* isn't the thing you're going for." He tossed his key on a tiny table with one chair and walked to the dresser beside the lone closet.

Nice to see he had a sense of humor hidden beneath that stony exterior. Other than a few terse commands about where to turn and park, their short trip from the floral shop had passed in silence, giving her plenty of time to second-guess the wisdom of forming this alliance with Jake Lonergan. It was sad, if not surprising, to see that he lived in such a Spartan abode. There was not one painting to give it color, no photograph to give any hint of what was important to Jake, no knickknack of any kind to give her any clue about her mysterious rescuer. There was certainly no sign of a family or that he ever entertained visitors, given the single chair and the sofa she suspected was there to serve as his bed rather than seating for guests. No wonder he lacked the social skills of other men she knew—he never got any practice socializing.

Is that what was he getting out of his agreement to help her and Emma? The chance to be a little less alone? He certainly didn't need her money, judging by the large roll of cash he pulled from the dresser. "You don't believe in banks?" she asked.

"I believe in being prepared." He stuffed the wad into the front pocket of his jeans.

"What are you preparing for?" she asked. "What do you think is going to happen?"

He'd charged to her rescue more than once, yet hid in the fringes of her life, avoiding contact with the police and almost anyone else. Beyond the striking silver-white hair and scars that she suspected made most people stare in morbid fascination or turn away in fear, he cursed and made cryptic comments. He shied away from holding a harmless baby, yet had no qualms about putting a stranglehold on an attacker. Maybe a few lessons in standard, polite behavior could be her gift to him—teaching him how to make friends, her way of thanking him. She might as well start with lesson number one. "It wouldn't kill you to answer a question when someone asks it."

"I don't know what's coming next, so I don't know what to say."

"'I don't know' is an answer," she pointed out. "It doesn't hurt you to just say so. And I won't feel like you're avoiding me again."

His eyes seemed particularly icy when they glanced at her. But he opened the closet door and shifted his attention there.

Robin tucked a strand of hair behind her ear and frowned at his broad back. Maybe friendship wasn't what he was hoping for, after all. While there'd been little familiarity with the process in that first kiss tonight, she'd been more sure of Jake's desire for her in those few moments he'd trapped her between the wall and his kiss than she'd been with Brian or any other man she'd been in a long-term relationship with. Besides, the man was a fast learner when he put his mind to it. She could count on one hand the number of times the memory of a kiss had stayed with her, and that greedy, grabby passion-fest tonight topped the list. Jake's overt masculinity triggered something ultra-feminine, vaguely nurturing and maybe just a little bit reckless inside her. She wasn't sure if she wanted to soften some of those rough edges and tutor him in the finer points of building a relationship, or if she wanted to throw caution to the wind and hold on for wherever the ride with Jake would take her.

Still, she knew next to nothing about the man. She sensed a horrible conflict inside him, and more secrets than most men had the strength to carry. He was armed and dangerous. Correction, he was dangerous even without being armed.

She shouldn't want him like she did. The overachiever in her shouldn't be toying with the idea of taming him, helping him deal with the demons that scarred his face and haunted his ice-blue eyes. She was certain to get burned, likely to fail. She shouldn't trust him. And yet, she'd placed her and Emma's lives in his hands. Whatever he wanted in return, whatever he needed, she vowed to give it willingly.

A week ago, Robin wouldn't have ventured into this neighborhood, just a few blocks from her shop, beyond the renovation of blighted downtown properties that Brian Elliott and other entrepreneurs were reclaiming. She certainly wouldn't have come here at night, with Emma in tow. Yet, with Jake walking by her side, she'd felt safe parking out front and carrying Emma into the old apartment building. These feelings about Jake were as irrational as they were deep. Maybe she should indulge the more practical side of her nature and get some answers to back up what her heart and soul were far too ready to believe—that he was a good man with a good heart, and that he would never knowingly hurt her or Emma.

"How long have you lived here?" she asked, trailing her finger across the counter and discovering that what the apartment lacked in personality, it made up for in cleanliness. That was a good sign, right? Or maybe it was a vigilant effort to hide something she should be seeing.

"Since I got the job at the Shamrock Bar." Jake pulled out a ratty leather satchel and stuffed a clean change of clothing inside. "I wanted a place within walking distance of work."

"You don't have a car?"

The bag clunked when he set it on the table, and Robin startled back a step. Whatever was inside was a lot heavier than some spare underwear. "Don't need one if I'm not going anyplace."

Surely, with all that cash she'd seen him stuff into the front pocket of his jeans, he could afford some kind of transportation. She tried not to dwell on what Detective Montgomery had said about how not being in the DMV database made Jake particularly hard to track. It had been a relief to learn he had no arrest record. But she still had no explanation for why he made such a concerted effort to hide from the world.

Curiosity had her peeking into the singed leather bag while he pulled a black hoodie from the closet. "What's in here? All your worldly possessions?"

"Robin, don't—"

Too late. "Oh, my God. What is all this?"

"I asked you not to look," he snapped.

Before Jake could zip the bag shut, she saw the cache of weaponry and reached inside. Curiosity instantly changed to fear. Or maybe that was anger.

"Don't yell at me," she chided. She picked up something that looked like a small hand grenade. "Why do you have these things?" She glanced over her shoulder to make sure Emma was still asleep in her carrier—as if shielding her daughter from the sight could shield her from the danger. "You can't have this arsenal around my daughter."

He plucked the grenade from her hand. "You already know I carry a knife and a gun."

"But all this? Are you expecting World War Three?" She'd seen boxes of bullets, a variety of knives and something that looked like pieces of a broken rifle. "This is crazy. I mean, is this even legal? Where did you get them? Do you know how to use them all?" Even as she said the words, she was waving the question aside and turning toward Emma. Of course he knew how to use them. That's why he didn't want to police to know who he was. That's why he hid from society. And she'd brought her baby here? "What kind of man are you?"

Jake opened the bag to replace the grenade thingee and stuffed the sweatshirt in beside it. "You're just now getting curious about who I am? After you sought me out and invited me into your life?"

"No, I've been curious all along, but I was respecting your privacy. It seemed so important to you." Robin picked up the carrier and headed to door. She was feeling anger, all right. Anger at herself for trusting her life to this enigma of a man for even one moment. It was disconcerting, too, to feel this sense of hurt. That could only mean she felt something for Jake, and caring for such a dangerous, difficult man made her a bigger fool yet. "This was a mistake."

"I thought you wanted a big, bad S.O.B."

She stopped with her hand on the knob and turned. He'd braced his hands on the tabletop, framing that bag of weapons with his shoulders, drilling her with those icy eyes and looking all kinds of intimidating. All Robin saw was the effort to shut her out. "I thought things had changed between us tonight. To find out you've been watching over us all along? That's…sweet."

"Sweet?" He sneered as if the word was a foreign concept to him.

"You must care on some level. And that kiss? That was more than— I don't let just anyone—" She tried to think of the right word to fit the tension simmering between them, and how this mysterious man had already gotten around her emotional defenses. But the words weren't there. The answers she needed weren't, either. "I think I have a right to know more about you. But every time I ask a question, you give me some cryptic response or nothing at all. I want to trust you, Jake. I thought I did. But the more I'm with you, the more I feel like an idiot for asking you to be our bodyguard."

Robin pulled open the door, but in two long strides, Jake was there to reach over her shoulder and shut it again.

"I'm sorry."

Robin held her breath, trying to ignore the way her skin leaped at the heat of his body standing so close to hers. She was as surprised by his apology as she'd been by his sudden movement across the room.

"I'm not used to people expecting something from me." He pulled his hand away from the door, reducing that feeling of being trapped. "You're not an idiot. You're a desperate woman, and I'm the kind of man who can cope with *desperate*. And you know it. If my word's worth anything, I promise you and Emma will be safe with me." His big fingers hovered in her peripheral vision, hesitating for a moment before touching her hair. It was almost a shy movement, infinitely gentle as he tucked the short brown waves behind her ear. "I need you to be safe. I've already got enough guilt on my conscience...." At his expectant pause, Robin tipped her chin to look up into those beautiful, striking blue eyes. "How do I get you to trust me?"

Her heart went out to his plea. Okay. She was willing to try this again. She reached up and cupped her hand against his clenched jaw. "Give me a straight answer?"

She could see he had to think about it. "May I?" With her nod of permission, he lifted the baby carrier from her arm and set it back on the counter. He gazed down at the sleeping infant, and for one endless moment, his hand floated over Emma, as if he wanted to touch her, too, but was afraid to. Instead, he curled his fingers into a fist and turned back to Robin. "What do you want to know?"

Robin hugged her arms around her waist, stopping herself from going to him and showing him that Emma wouldn't break beneath a caress as gentle as the way he'd stroked her own hair. "What's your aversion to common civility and human kindness?"

Jake shook his head. "I can protect you, Robin. The kid, too. But this is how I work. I'm not a nice guy."

"If you weren't a nice guy, you wouldn't be so good with my baby."

He shrugged off the compliment and held out his hand. "Give me your keys. Tomorrow morning we'll need to switch your rental to a truck or SUV that I don't have to crawl out of, and that has a thicker chassis to offer us better protection."

She didn't try to mask her frustrated sigh. "You're

doing it again. You didn't answer my question. What kind of mother trusts her family to a man who's armed to the teeth and won't answer a simple question?"

"What you're asking isn't simple."

"Then I'll give you another chance." Robin crossed to him, demanding the truth, any truth, that seemed so hard for him to give. "Why should I give you the keys to my car? Detective Montgomery said you don't have a driver's license."

"Just because I don't own a car doesn't mean I don't know how to drive." Robin didn't budge an inch at the flippant reply. After a brief stare-down, Jake muttered a curse and circled around the table to unzip his bag and pull out a small plastic card from one of the inside pockets. "Here."

She took the card he handed across the table. A driver's license. State of Missouri. Current. So why had it been so hard for him to give a straight answer? And then she read the tiny print more carefully. "This says Ken Edscorn." She looked up at the inscrutable mask on his face. "Did you used to live in St. Louis? Did you change your name?"

"I don't know."

"You don't know?" He pulled another license from the bag and handed it to her. Now she was even more confused. "Otto Lundgren?"

He reached for the licenses, but Robin turned her back on him to study the cards more carefully. "This is you." The same face as the man behind her, with longer, darker hair and no scar at the temple, stared back at her. "These are both you. I don't understand."

"Neither do I."

She spun around. "What kind of answer...?" Jake held up a placating hand and she bit her tongue, giving him a chance to explain.

"There are six different IDs in this bag. Jake isn't even

one of them. It's a name I picked because I thought it went with Lonergan." He paused, pressed his mouth into a grim line, then exhaled a quick breath. "And it's easy to remember."

"Easy to remember?"

"I, um…" he touched the scar in his scalp "…have gaps in my memory."

She pulled her gaze from the ridge of scar tissue that bespoke some injury to his brain. "Gaps?"

"One big gap. I'm missing a whole lifetime." He nodded toward the cards in her hand. "I don't know if I'm Ken, Otto or someone else." He dropped his hand on top of the black leather bag. "But I know how to use these things. Better than any man should. I know how to keep someone safe."

"You have amnesia?"

"I was shot in the head. Two years ago I woke up in a Texas hospital in some no-name border town with this bag and no memory of the man I used to be."

"Oh, Jake. How awful." She hurried back to the table and lay her hand over his. When he turned his hand to capture hers, she squeezed him just as tightly. She stroked her thumb across his knuckles, offering him what comfort she could. "Why are you hiding away from the world? Why aren't you out beating the bushes, trying locate your family or friends? Somebody has to be missing you."

His thumb mimicked the same caress across the back of her hand. "There was nobody at my bedside in that hospital. No cards, no flowers. I've never once seen my face on a missing person news story. Nobody's looking for me. Nobody I want to meet, at any rate. Every now and then I think somebody's watching me and I move on. For all I know, Otto Lundgren or any of those other aliases could be a criminal wanted by the police. Or by some other lowlife."

"Why would you think…?" She looked at his damaged face and down at the weapons cache beneath their joined hands and understood.

"Told you I wasn't Prince Charming." He let her pull away. He splayed his fingers at his waist, thickening his biceps and shoulders, and looking every bit the dangerous man he believed he was—the fugitive from the law he might well be. "Still want my protection?"

Robin turned away to watch her daughter sleep. She tucked the cotton blanket up beneath Emma's chin and brushed a finger along one precious, chubby cheek. So Jake, or whoever he was, had amnesia. Did she risk her daughter's life, and possibly her own heart, on a man who might have done something horrible in a life he couldn't remember? Or did she believe in the man he was now? She stroked Emma's cheek again. "Have you done anything bad—hurt anyone—that you *can* remember?"

"Stopped a guy from raping a woman one night."

Turning at the deep, husky statement, Robin searched those uniquely handsome eyes for the reassurance she needed. "You won't let anything happen to my daughter?"

Jake stood there, silent, imposing—showing her with his stance and demeanor that that had been a question he didn't need to answer.

With her decision made, Robin crossed back to the table and handed him the licenses. "Then I don't care who you used to be. You're the man I need now." She picked up the carrier while Jake slung the heavy bag over his shoulder and followed her to the door. "And I know we're an imposition, so I'm going to repay you."

"No, you're not."

"Hot meal. Comfy bed. It's what people do when some-one helps them."

He locked the door behind them and followed her down the hallway to the elevator. "Robin, that's not neces—"

"I want you to talk to me, too. If you don't know the answer, say so. But you have to try."

"I still need your keys."

She pushed the call button and fished the ring of keys from her pocket. "And I'm still calling you Jake."

"Does anyone ever win an argument with you?"

"I don't know." The old bronze doors separated and she stepped inside. She made sure he was looking at her before she dropped the keys into his palm. "You'll have to keep trying."

Chapter Nine

Jake was screwed. He'd exchanged his stark downtown haunts where he knew every alley and fire escape, every place trouble could hide, for the domestic mousetrap of Robin's rambling brick farmhouse on the outskirts of the city.

The twentieth-century home had more doors and windows than one man could watch at any one time. They'd been updated with new locks, but there were a detached garage, a barn and a gardening shed he'd need to keep an eye on, too. Plus, sight lines didn't allow him much of a heads-up to anyone approaching the house on foot. While Robin didn't run the place as a working farm, there were still rolling grass hills between the house and the highway, as well as a forest of native pines and deciduous trees running along her property to the south and east.

Despite its remote location away from the incidents around her downtown shop, her home would be a nightmare for one man to defend, even if he were at the top of his game. Jake was far too distracted tonight to be at the top of anything.

First, there was the house. Even at night, its tree-lined drive appealed to his need for isolation in a much prettier way than the lumpy sofa bed, thrift-shop table and tight space of his apartment did. Then there was the food.

Robin had claimed she could cook, but leftover stew and banana-nut muffins shouldn't taste like the best meal he'd eaten in two long years.

Finally, there was Robin herself. She'd kicked off her shoes as soon as she got inside the house and ran around in her bare toes and butt-hugging jeans, somehow managing to pull off sexy while she heated up some dinner and gave Emma her bath. Every room of the house was a reflection of some aspect of her—practical and efficient, stylish and comfortable, beautiful in a subtle, take-a-man-by-surprise kind of way.

He liked it all. He liked her.

If he stayed here too long, he'd get soft and be useless as the protector Robin and Emma needed. He was equally certain that the moment he dropped his guard would be the moment that his past caught up with him. And whether he remembered the details or not, he doubted the reunion would be a pleasant one. Being with Robin and Emma would put them right in the middle of whatever dangers were lying in wait for him.

After another late-night sweep to make sure every door and window was locked, Jake wandered into the nursery, where Robin was cleaning up after putting Emma down in her crib. The dim light from the lamp on the dresser and the soft strains of classical music playing in the background made Jake drop his voice to a whisper. "Everything is as secure as I can make it."

"Thank you." Robin's voice was just as quiet. She stifled a yawn before gathering up a towel and the clothes Emma had been wearing earlier. "I'll get your room ready next."

He was about to tell her not to go to any trouble on his behalf when a little whimpering noise came from the crib. Jake crossed the room to look down at the pink, squirming ball of Emma Carter. Her eyes were closed, but she was batting at the gingham sheet beneath her, pinching her face and moaning like she was gearing up to cry. "Is she okay?"

"Of course. Full tummy, warm bath. She'll be asleep in no time." Robin was folding up the Noah's ark quilt that had been tossed over the rocking chair where she'd given Emma her bottle.

"Then why is she crying?"

"She's not. She's stubborn like her mama and fighting to stay awake." Another yawn betrayed Robin's fatigue and the late hour. She needed to get to bed. They all needed to get some sleep if they were going to stay sharp and vigilant against any other threats. "Just nudge her thumb to her mouth. She never took a pacifier, but sucking her thumb seems to calm her right down."

"You want me touch her?"

Robin warmed the room with a smile. "Of course. She won't bite."

Jake was a grown man who outweighed little Emma by at least two hundred pounds. Still, he needed a fortifying breath before he reached over the oak railing and caught one of Emma's tiny fists between two of his fingers. He guided the hand to her mouth. As soon as it touched her lips, the thumb popped right in and the unhappy noises stopped. And she did it all without opening her eyes. "That's my girl."

Entranced by the scent of baby powder and innocence, Jake splayed his hand across Emma's tummy and got a little choked up in the wonder of how warm she was beneath the soft lavender sleeper she wore. Even his big, callused hand could feel her tiny lungs expanding and contracting, and her heart beating at a strong, even pace beneath his fingertips.

Oh, man. His boss, Robbie, was right. Jake *was* smitten with little Emma Carter.

He was distracted enough by the unfamiliar tumble of emotions that he didn't hear Robin move up beside him until she spoke. "You're good with her. You're especially gentle."

Jake pulled his hand away to wrap it around the top of the crib rail. "I figure I have to be. I don't always know my own strength."

She slid her hand over Jake's and the emotions bombarding him almost made it hard to breathe. Her soft question echoed his own thoughts. "Do you think you ever had any children, Jake? Any nieces or nephews to dote on?"

"I don't know," he answered honestly. But if he felt this pull, this protective vibe about a child he'd only known for a week, wouldn't he have some sense of those same feelings about a child of his own—even if he couldn't recall a name or face? "I doubt it. The kid here seems as foreign to me as she is beautiful."

"She is, isn't she?" Robin reached over to smooth that thick, dark hair off Emma's forehead. "Beautiful, I mean."

"Nobody's going to hurt her, Robin." He laced their fingers together and looked down over the jut of his shoulder at her. Good guy or bad guy, he felt that promise deep in his bones. "I won't let anyone take her from you."

With a slight nod, she tugged on his hand and led the way out of the room. Once in the hallway, she turned to the right while Jake pulled the door to behind them. "I'll put you in the room next door where my parents stay when they visit."

Jake released her hand and headed in the opposite direction, back to the room with the flat-screen television and stone fireplace. "I saw an easy chair in here that'll do for tonight."

Even with those silent bare feet, he sensed her changing course and hurrying after him. "You can't stay awake twenty-four hours a day. None of the threats or calls have come to the house. I think it's okay to drop your guard for a little bit here."

"Are you in the phone book?" He picked up his go-bag off the red-and-white-checked couch and looked for a better spot to stash it.

"Yes."

"Then it wouldn't take a rocket scientist to track you down." He saw the slightly hidden yet easy-access spot under the big square coffee table and stuffed it underneath. "It's probably only a matter of time before your perp escalates his game and brings the threat here."

"You're doing it again—talking all doom and gloom like there's no hope in the world."

Robin stood at the edge of the couch, hugging herself in that nervous way that made him want to wrap her up in his arms and promise everything would be all right. But his concentration was already compromised by the difficult admission of his amnesia—a self-reliant secret he hadn't shared with anyone in K.C. Then there was that fairy-tale interlude he'd just had in the nursery with Emma.

No connections. No commitments. No caring.

The Carter girls had blown the philosophy that had served him so well these past two years right out of the water. If he wanted to recapture the fighting edge that made him such a ruthless survivor, he needed to nip all this touchy-feely normalcy in the bud. "You want comfort, talk to your girlfriends. You want protection, I'm your man."

"Hope for the best, but prepare for the worst? Is that how a man like you thinks?"

She deserved an honest answer. "There isn't always hope. But I can always be prepared."

Her skin paled at the bleak response. But she'd made him promise to keep talking, even if she didn't like what he had to say. "What made you such a hard, unsociable man, Jake? Who hurt you?"

The pity in that question took him by surprise. He'd always thought of himself as the monster dealing out the pain. That was the story his nightmares told. He'd gotten so used to believing he was the bad guy that it was a challenge to consider he might not always have been this way. "You think I know? Say good-night to Sunshine in there and get to bed. If I get too tired, I'll sack out on the couch."

"I have guest rooms."

Un-uh. A bed would feel too cozy. Too normal. And protecting the Carter girls from whoever was threatening them required those skills that normal men didn't possess. "I'd rather be between you two and the front door in case something happens."

"All right." Giving up her insistence on civility, Robin left the room. She came back a minute later with pillows, sheets and a quilt. She unfolded one of the sheets to cover the couch, and set the rest of the bedding on top, letting him decide just how civilized he wanted to be tonight. "I owe you more than you can know for the peace of mind you give me by being here. Someday I hope you'll let me repay…" A clear conscience was the only payment he'd asked for, and this time she let the subject die. "I know. Good night."

After a moment's hesitation, she circled the coffee table, braced her hand at the center of his chest and stretched up on tiptoe to press a soft, gentle kiss to his lips. Her eyes sought out his before she gave him another kiss, just as tender, just as sweet. It was the gentlest, most beautiful touch he could remember and he couldn't help but move his lips against hers.

As raw and passionate as that kiss at her shop had been, this one warmed and healed. The sweet, soothing connection tamed something raw inside him. It pulled him from the lonely curse he'd lived with for far too long. When the first sizzle of heat entered the kiss, Robin dropped to her heels and pulled away.

"Good night, Jake."

Yeah. He wanted more than the satisfaction of knowing he'd done all he could to help these two damsels in distress. He wanted a thousand more kisses like that. He wanted to learn how to change a diaper. He wanted what other men had—a good woman, a beautiful child. Laughter. Love. A real home. But he wasn't other men. So he let Robin walk to her room and close the door without voicing the wishes stirring in his heart.

THE NIGHTMARE HAD him at its mercy again.

Wheezing through the pain that seared him inside and out, Jake crouched in the darkness. "You have to stop him."

A hazy apparition moved in the shadows, a faceless threat he had to destroy. He flipped the knife into his hand and hurled it. With a choking scream, the apparition sank into the darkness.

Just like that, his enemy was dead. But there were other threats in the shadows. If he couldn't find them all, people would die. He'd seen so much death. He couldn't survive another.

"Jake?"

He heard the soft voice calling to him through the mists and death of his dream.

"Robin." He had to save her.

He couldn't think through the heat and the pain, couldn't claw his way out of the darkness to get to her.

"Don't hurt her." Now the gun was in his hand and he was running. His lungs were burning, his shoulder bleeding. He wasn't fast enough.

He wiped the sweat from his eyes and caught a glimpse of pale skin and rich brown hair. She reached out to him, but those sweet, gray-blue eyes were so afraid.

"Jake?"

Shadows from every corner of his mind rushed at her, knocked her down, consumed her. "Robin!"

He raised his gun, stroked his finger against the trigger. But he had no target. He was losing her. He was too late. He couldn't save her.

"Ken?"

The darkness exploded around him. Fire seared through his flesh. Terror ripped through his heart. He moaned through his despair.

She was gone. Everything that mattered was gone.

And then he heard the baby crying. He crawled toward the sound. He peered into the flames of his burning world and saw the shadows again, emerging, one by one, darting toward that heartbreaking cry.

Jake pushed to his feet. They couldn't have her. He was the man who saved people. He couldn't fail again.

"Otto? Please."

He followed the baby's cries through the flames and the darkness. "I'm coming," he muttered. "I'm coming."

He reached the shadows and dove into the heart of their blackness. They shifted their target and came at him— pummeling, pulling, cutting, killing.

"Go," he whispered, taking on death itself to save that innocent life. "Be safe."

"Lonergan!"

Jake came awake on a voiceless roar and lunged at his attackers. He caught one by the shoulders and flipped him to the ground beneath him.

"Jake!"

He knew that voice. Not a threat, but a hope. A wish. He shook his head to clear the shadows from his mind and orient himself in the hazy darkness. Red-and-white checks. Short, dark hair. He blinked. "Robin?"

He blinked again and saw her slender body pinned to her sofa by his big hands and lower body. He saw the fading bruise on her collarbone peeking out beneath the baby-blue pajama top she wore and feared he'd just put similar marks on her.

"Are you okay?" she whispered, brushing her fingertips against his bare, damp chest. She was petting him again, taming the instinctive fight response out of him while he...

"Oh, hell. Oh, honey..." Jake swore at what he'd done, at the violence that seemed to be a part of every heartbeat. He shifted his hips off hers and sat up, scooting to the far end of the couch. "I'm sorry. I'm so sorry."

He tried to push to his feet, but she got up on her knees and threw her arms around his neck before he could stand. "You can't run and hide this time." Her knees found a spot on either side of his left thigh and she pulled herself against his chest, sliding her soft cheek against his and hugging him close. "You're all right. It was a nightmare. Let's deal with it. Let's face this together. You're all right."

"I hurt you." He gripped the back and arm of the couch, fighting what his body wanted to do. "I didn't mean..." And then her warmth and strength and stubborn spirit moved past the guilt and fear, and Jake wound his arms around her, squeezing her tight. "Oh, God, honey, I need..." He needed the warm human contact to ground himself back in reality. "I just need to hold you. Can I hold you?"

She nodded, rubbing her cheek against his. "It's okay. You're safe."

"Safe?" He swiped at the tears that stung his eyes and buried his face in the fragrant softness of her hair. "*I'm* supposed to protect *you*."

Her palms slid up against his scalp and across his back, wrapping him up in her shielding strength. "You're not going to win this argument. Just talk to me."

He almost laughed at the idea of her bossing him around. But it had been too long since he'd laughed, too long since he'd shared any part of himself with another person.

She pressed a kiss against his grizzled cheek and pulled back enough to stroke her fingers beside his eyes and beside his mouth. "Your face was contorted in such pain. You were thrashing and moaning. You scared me."

"I'm sorry." He leaned forward and stole a quick kiss. "I didn't mean to. Usually, I just deal…" Her hands settled atop his shoulders and she waited expectantly for him to continue. "That's why I was there that first night you were attacked." He reached down to pull her legs from around his and settled her squarely on his lap. "I'd had a nightmare, and I thought a cold, long walk in the rain would clear my head. At first I thought…" He tangled his fingers into her sleep-mussed hair and tucked it behind her ear. "When I heard you scream, for a split second I was reliving…something. I had to save you. I've got this thing about saving people."

"I know." Her hands never left his skin; her gaze never left his face. "Was it the same nightmare tonight?"

Jake nodded. She asked a question—he tried to answer. That was the deal. Every time Robin forced him a little closer toward that civilized behavior she kept insisting on, the easier it became. "In my dreams, I have to kill someone or I'll be killed."

"Who?"

"I don't know. I'm killing shadows—stabbing, shooting, strangling with my bare hands—any way I can." She gasped softly at the graphic images he described, but let him continue. "I think I'm saving lives but maybe I'm just saving my own skin. Either way, I'm failing. I'm bleeding. I'm…"

"Do you think it's a memory trying to surface?"

"It sure feels real." He clenched his teeth so tight against the images he'd seen that the muscles in his jaw were shaking. "You and Emma were there tonight, mixed up in all the violence. I couldn't save you."

"Oh, Jake." She squirmed against his groin, waking something far more basic than the gentle warmth she stirred in other parts of his body as she lay her head on his shoulder and wound her arms around his waist. He felt the bead of a firm breast brush across his skin and every muscle she leaned against quivered in response. "Shh. We're okay. Both of us are okay."

Jake didn't want to be feeling this desire heating his blood. Robin was lean and soft, wearing cotton pajamas that were far too thin for her not to notice the swelling response of all this touching and talking and tenderness. He pulled his fingers from her hair and set her on the rumpled sheet beside him. He pushed to his feet and stalked across the room, scrubbing his hand over his face. "I damn near snapped you in two. How is that okay?"

"I'm still here, Jake. I'm in one piece. I think you must have some kind of post-traumatic stress. I know you didn't mean it." He silently cursed the face reflected in the mirror above the empty fireplace. But Robin came right after him. She pulled his hand back to her cheek and turned her face into his palm. "I'm not any part of your nightmare. I'm real. I'm now."

With that much of an invitation, his fingers inevitably wound into the silky waves of her hair. "I wish I could remember. The doctors said with an injury like mine, the memories sometimes never come back." The moon outside filtered through the windows, casting a cool light over her beautiful face. "I wish I knew if I was a good guy who deserved you, or some murdering S.O.B. you need to be running from."

"I can't imagine what that's like, to have lost so much of yourself. But I do know this. To me, you're Jake Lonergan. You're the man who saved my life and my daughter's. And that makes you a very good guy in my book."

"But what if—"

She pressed her fingers over his lips and cut off his argument. "No what-ifs. Only certainties tonight, okay? Maybe you'll never get your past back. But you have the present. And you have a future. A man gets to choose who he wants to be every day of his life. Decide who you want to be right now. Choose to be a hero. Choose to be with us. Forget about whether or not you killed someone, whether you did it out of self-defense or... Oh." A pink blush stained her cheeks as she pulled her hand away with an apology. "*Forget* was a poor choice of words but—"

Jake cupped her face between his hands, pulled her onto her toes and kissed her. Hard. She tumbled into his chest and he kissed her again. "I get it. I choose you." He thrust his tongue into her mouth, surrendering to her stubborn faith in him, claiming the compassion and understanding she gave. "I choose here. Now."

Her lips chased after his, parted, welcomed. He took anything she offered, and damn, the woman was generous. She braced her hands against his chest and curled her fingertips into his skin, igniting ten hot spots of desire that fed the need simmering deeper inside him.

"I need you, Robin." One more kiss and his body was just as hot as it had been during the throes of that nightmare, but in a very different, much more pleasurable way. "I need to hold on to you. And reality." She nodded, understanding, and Jake swung her up into his arms and carried her back to the sofa. "I need you."

"Yes."

The single word was a gift he didn't deserve, but one he needed to hear as he laid her on the overstuffed cushions and slid on top of her. His jeans and shorts were uncomfortably tight and he couldn't help but rub against the juncture of her thighs. She held on to his neck and kissed his throat, his jaw, the corner of his mouth, fueling the fire that was already burning dangerously beyond his control.

Jake pushed up the hem of her shirt, running his hands over her smooth skin, exposing her pretty breasts to the moonlight and feasting his eyes on the tight, rosy peaks. "I need you to keep the nightmares away."

"This is you and me. We're real. I want—" He closed his hungry mouth over her breast, suckled the pebbled tip against his tongue and she bucked beneath him, gasping his name.

Oh, damn. He'd hurt her.

"It's too much, isn't it. Too intense." Denying his own raging need, he pushed himself up, carefully pulling his body away from hers. "You don't have to do this. I can take a cold shower."

"Don't you dare." With a determination that shouldn't have surprised him, Robin pushed him against the back of the sofa and climbed into his lap. She straddled his arousal and reached for the hem of her pajama top, stripping it off over her head and shaking her hair loose around her face as she tossed the shirt aside. She was the most glorious thing he'd ever seen. "I need you, too. I've been on my own a long time, Jake. It's hard to be alone—even if you can manage it. And I've never been drawn to anyone the way I'm drawn to you."

He groaned at the need pulsing through him and fisted his hands on the couch. "I haven't been with a woman since... I can't remember."

She reached for his hands and placed them over her breasts, showing him with her body that he hadn't hurt her at all. "Then we'll rediscover how it's done—together."

There were no more words and not nearly the finesse this woman deserved. In a flurry of bumping hands and stolen kisses, they shed the rest of their clothes. He found a condom in his go-bag and she rolled it onto him. Jake palmed two handfuls of her round, beautiful bottom and lifted her over his lap, nudging at her entrance before pushing into her tight, welcoming heat.

Her fingers dug into his shoulders as he moved beneath her, sliding in faster, deeper—growing impossibly harder with every feverish thrust. He captured her nipple in his mouth again and drew on her until she moaned his name and her moist sheath began to spasm around him.

"Jake." She leaned back, rocking her hips against his. He palmed her breast, tunneled his fingers into her hair. "Jake." He tightened his grip around her buttocks and thighs, anchoring her to him as he thrust up inside her. Everything in him rushed to the spot where they were joined—all the guilt, all the doubt, all the need, all the fire. He could scarcely breathe. He could barely think. But he could look. He could feel. Her body gripped him like a firm, urging hand and he shook with his release deep inside her. "Jake!"

He'd never forget the wondrous look in her eyes as she flew apart in his arms.

He'd never forget her cuddling close as he stretched out on the sofa and pulled her down beside him afterward. He spread the quilt over them both as their bodies cooled, and he savored the skin-to-skin trust of Robin dozing off beside him.

He'd never forget how right and humbling and perfect it felt to be fully in the here and now, making new memories with Robin to store in his mind and heart.

"You need to sleep, too," she whispered some time later, perhaps sensing that he'd been awake, trailing lazy circles along her hip, watching over her. She snugged that perfect little bottom against the cradle of his thighs and laced her fingers together with his, pulling his arm across her stomach. "Were you thinking about the nightmare again?"

Jake ignored the leaping impulses of his body, waking again at the intimate contact. There was something more than sex he needed from Robin tonight. He needed the peace this woman brought to his fractured mind. He needed the light she brought to his frozen heart. He needed to be the man—that good man—she believed he could be.

"No." Jake pulled her hair aside and pressed a kiss behind her ear. "Can we hear Emma in here if she wakes up?"

Robin nodded. "I brought the monitor with me when I came to check on you."

"Good." He nuzzled the nape of her neck. "Because I don't think I'm a strong enough man to let you go right now."

"I'm not going anywhere, Jake. Promise me you won't…go anywhere, either."

He could guess she wasn't just talking about staying with her physically. "I'll do my best."

After checking to make sure his knife was beneath the pillow, and his gun was within easy reach beneath the coffee table, Jake let his eyes drift shut. With his body sated and Robin tucked safely against him, he slept through the rest of the night.

Chapter Ten

Jake pulled a T-shirt on over his jeans and reached for the pair of socks he'd laid out on the sofa. "Hey, you." One of the socks had tumbled over the side onto the blanket where Emma lay beneath an arched baby entertainment center. But instead of batting at the plastic animals dangling overhead, she'd found the plain white sock and was noshing on that as if it was her favorite toy. "Trade you."

He knelt down to gently pry the sock from her fingers. She fussed a little, and while he was beginning to learn that the soft coos and protesting noises were just her way of communicating, Jake still got a knot in his stomach at the sound of distress and quickly guided her hands up to the blue cat hanging over her head. When she buzzed her lips in satisfaction, Jake smiled.

Jake Lonergan, babysitter. Not a job title he ever would have imagined for himself.

He tilted his head toward the soft humming coming from the shower in the master bedroom. "Your mama's pretty skin must be pruning by now. Good thing you and I ate breakfast before she got in there."

Emma's blue eyes looked right at him and he imagined her smile was a "yes" to his conversation. With the Carter girls both temporarily occupied, Jake finished dressing.

He'd already showered and come back to the family

room in his shorts and jeans to watch Robin sleep for a few minutes until he heard Emma fussing over the baby monitor and he'd leaned down to wake Robin with a kiss. He could see she was tired, despite a smile and a "Good morning."

If surviving his nightmare and a round of lovemaking with him on a couch didn't wear a woman out, then single parenting did. She'd pushed her hair out of her eyes and glanced at the antique clock on the mantel with a weary sigh. "Is she awake already?"

Jake heard the words coming out of his own mouth even before he'd fully thought them through. "If you get a bottle ready for her and trust me to change a diaper, I'll feed Emma breakfast while you take a bath or whatever you need to do."

"Really?" Robin had sat right up, clutching the sheet to her naked breasts. "A long, hot, private shower where I don't have to have Emma in her carrier in the bathroom with me? You'd do that?"

"If you trust me with her."

"Always." Robin had gathered the sheet around her like a sarong, stretched up to kiss him and run down the hallway to the nursery before he fully comprehended what his offer might mean to the woman.

"Take your time," he'd called after her. A man couldn't turn down a response like that any more than he'd been able to turn down Robin's whispered request a couple hours earlier. She'd rolled over on the sofa just before sunrise and asked if he had another condom in his bag. Making love that second time had been slower, sweeter, saner, yet no less earthshaking than that first wild ride on the sofa had been.

For a man who didn't want to care about anything or

have any connections to anyone, he was already in pretty deep with these two.

The phone in Robin's kitchen rang before he got the first sock on. With a quick glance down the hallway to verify that the water was still running in the shower, he got up and went to the kitchen to answer it. "Yeah?"

"Is this the Carter residence?" The man's voice sounded familiar, but Jake wasn't taking any chances that this was one of those harassing phone calls like Robin had received at her shop.

"Who's asking?"

"Spencer Montgomery, KCPD." Jake carried the cordless receiver back to the family room so he could keep an eye on Emma. "I take it this is Mr. Lonergan?"

"Yeah." He didn't bother explaining why he was at Robin's home this early in the morning. Nor was he going to tell the detective that she'd been soaking in the shower for the past twenty minutes. "She isn't available right now. Can I take a message?"

"Actually, I'm looking for you."

Spencer Montgomery didn't strike Jake as a man who did polite chitchat, either. "What do you need, detective?"

"I just got a call from the DEA asking about you. The database search I ran on you flagged in their system." Jake pulled out his beat-up black satchel and unzipped the pocket that held the badge with J. Lonergan emblazoned on it. "Your picture in the morning paper put you on somebody's desk."

"Morning paper?" Jake slipped the badge into his jeans pocket and opened the *Kansas City Journal* that he'd pulled from Robin's mailbox during his early morning reconnaissance of the place.

"Check page three. You're getting to be a regular legend in the city." Yeah, like a Bigfoot sighting.

Jake tucked the phone between his shoulder and ear and spread the paper open on the coffee table. "Ah, hell."

There he was, in black and white. The bastard who'd taken his picture from the speeding car must have been Gabriel Knight. Or someone who'd sold the picture to the reporter. *Is this the city's unsung hero?*

The detective gave him a few seconds to let the image and caption below it sink in. "Looks like the Ghost Rescuer has finally been unmasked. Although it doesn't look like Gabe Knight got a very flattering picture of you."

There were no flattering pictures of him. Jake quickly skimmed the article. Still no name listed, but if a blurry, nighttime photograph was enough for Spencer Montgomery to recognize him, then it wasn't unreasonable to suspect that someone who knew him well would recognize him, too. It wasn't exactly a forgettable face. Worse yet, with Robin's Nest Floral Shop painted on the awning behind him, they'd know exactly where to come find him.

Or who they could use to get to him.

Jake closed the paper and pushed to his feet again. "Who called from the DEA?"

"A Charlie Nash. You know him?"

Jake tried to envision a name and a face. But all he came up with were blanks. "No."

The running water at the back of the house finally stopped. He could imagine Robin's sleek, wet body stepping out of the shower. He could see her pale skin blushing pink as she toweled herself dry from head to toe. She was a practical, cotton pajama kind of woman, but he couldn't imagine anything sexier than Robin Carter naked.

And now he had to leave her.

That would be what the cagey, self-preserving survivor in him would do. The DEA knew he was in Kansas City?

Then he had to go. If he was on the DEA's radar, he must be wanted for something.

Emma squealed at his feet, excited by the red and blue animals swinging over her head. Jake knelt down beside her to still the hanging toys. She batted at his big finger and he turned it into her palm, letting her latch on and pull it to her mouth for a sweet, slobbery lick. She buzzed her lips against his skin and they both smiled.

Right. Like he could leave this one alone and unprotected with a clear conscience.

A sense of inevitable doom sank like a rock in Jake's gut. The violence from his past was closing in, and now these two women might get caught in the retribution for whatever horrible things he'd done.

"Agent Nash says he's flying in later today from Houston. He wants to meet with you."

Montgomery had to be giving him a heads-up for a reason. Maybe he was fishing for information, too. "Did he say why?"

"Nash said it had to do with an investigation he couldn't discuss with me." Jake stood at the detective's telling pause. "Why would the DEA be interested in you, Mr. Lonergan?"

"I honestly don't know."

Jake pulled out the badge and traced his thumb over the letters that could have been carved in Cyrillic, for as much as they meant to him. He considered the passports in his bag that said he'd been in and out of the country several times—to countries with known drug trafficking. A tough guy—a killer—like him would be just the kind of enforcer any one of those cartels hired. His chest hurt. Two weeks ago, news like this would have sent him packing to a new town where he could hide until whoever was tracking him lost their lead and gave up.

But two weeks ago, he had no ties to anyone. Two weeks ago, he hadn't given his word that he'd keep the Carter girls safe.

Two weeks ago, he hadn't been in love.

Ah, hell.

"Lonergan?"

"I'm here."

"Does Robin Carter know what kind of man you are?"

After yesterday and last night, he didn't suppose there were any more secrets between them. "Yeah."

"Do I need to advise you to walk away?"

"Wouldn't do you any good." If the DEA could track him down, that meant others could, too. It also meant that whoever was terrorizing Robin might become harder to identify if there were more than one threat circling around them. "Montgomery?"

"Yes?"

"I promised Robin I'd provide protection for her until these threats stop and you catch the man who attacked her."

"I'm listening."

"If something should happen to me, would you be willing to supply back-up? I need to know they'll be safe."

The detective held things pretty close to the vest, so it was hard to get a good read on whether he was an ally or an enemy. But Jake was betting that Montgomery would put solving his case ahead of whatever suspicions he might have about Jake. "You can call me. I have a feeling Ms. Carter is important to our task force investigation."

"Thanks."

"What should I tell Agent Nash when he shows up?"

"Tell him I'm busy."

Jake disconnected the call and set the phone on the

coffee table. He pulled out his go-bag and armed himself. Knife. Gun. Spare magazine in his pocket.

"Jake? Did I hear the phone?" Robin appeared at the end of the hallway, wrapped up in a fuzzy white robe and towel drying her hair. "Has something happened?"

"Are you sure you have to work that wedding today?"

She draped the towel over her shoulder and went straight to Emma to pick her up. She hugged the baby protectively against her chest. "It's my job. The Vanderhams are good customers. You didn't answer my question. Did the person who's been harassing me find my home number?"

Thus far, the sicko calling Robin and sending her those threats had acted anonymously. Even the night she'd been assaulted, and when she'd been locked inside that refrigerator, the coward had waited until she was alone to attack. Surely, he wouldn't change his MO now and try something with all the people who would be around her at a wedding.

"No." He threaded the knife sheath onto his belt while she waited for an explanation. He'd promised to answer her questions, but wasn't sure if telling her the DEA was now looking for him would inspire the kind of trust he needed from her if the threat escalated and he needed to take action to keep her and Emma safe. He opted for a half truth. "Detective Montgomery called while you were in the shower."

"Did he find the man who attacked me?"

"Not yet. But he did stress that you were important to his case. He wanted to make sure you had sufficient protection."

"I have you. Right?"

Damn straight. He tucked the Beretta into the back of his belt, wanting quicker access to it than what the ankle holster allowed. "Can you take care of Emma now?"

"Of course."

"Good." He dropped a hard, far-too-brief kiss on her mouth and headed for front door. "Then I'm going to walk the grounds and check the car, make sure everything's as secure as it needs to be while you get dressed."

She and Emma followed him right to the door. "You're doing it again. What did Detective Montgomery say? Why are you arming yourself like this?"

"You can't change a man overnight, Robin." As soon as the harsh tone left his mouth, Jake regretted it. He pulled his hand from the doorknob and touched her damp hair, apologizing. "You can't...fix me. I got a feeling something bad is coming. You have to let me do what I know how to do."

"Over here, Leon." Robin waved the man carrying the second part of the Vanderhams' altar arrangement up to the front of the church. The younger man tilted his head to peek through the stand of red and white roses to find the step, and Robin hurried down to help him. She grabbed one end of the arrangement's brass base and helped him steer around the pulpit. "This goes inside the ring I've already set up. Careful."

He heaved it onto the center of the altar. "Don't let those cascading ones get caught underneath."

"Got it." It took several more minutes to make sure all the flowers were set properly. Robin pulled out a couple of broken red stems. "We'll need to replace these. Run out to the van and bring in the box of spares."

"Um…" Leon nervously ran his fingers inside the collar of his uniform. "There's nothing else in the van. I must have forgotten that box."

"You forgot? I specifically wrote that down on the manifest. How many things have to disappear before—?" A muted rumble of thunder rattled the stained-glass windows and Robin shivered. Lordy, she was jumpy today. And she was already running behind schedule setting up for the ceremony.

"I'm sorry, ma'am. Do you want me to drive back to the shop and get some?"

Robin eased a calming breath through her nose. "No, I'm sorry. There isn't time for that." She glanced over at Emma in her carrier on the first pew, sleeping peacefully through the hubbub. Oh, to be stress-free like that right now. She turned to Leon and apologized again for snapping at him. "We'll make do."

True, setting up for the Vanderhams' renewal ceremony required a lot of work in a short time frame, but that wasn't why she was so short-tempered this afternoon. She glanced to the back of the church where Jake stood outside in the lobby by the front doors, keeping an eye on both the interior and exterior of the building. Beyond the church's open front door, the overcast sky threatened rain, driving some early arrivals inside the lobby, where they mingled, waiting until her staff cleared the sanctuary. More people for Jake to watch and worry about, she supposed. Maybe that explained the grim impatience lining his features.

His ice-blue gaze met hers. He held up his wrist and pointed to his watch. Right. He was antsy about something she was certain he hadn't shared with her. That hyperalertness made her edgy, too. Maybe she should give Detective Montgomery a call to find out just what he had discussed with Jake to send him into commando mode.

She turned back to Leon and smiled. "I'll pull stems out of the back and fill in where they'll show in the wedding pictures." What was one missing box of long-stemmed red roses, anyway? In her mind, the decorations already looked like the floral blanket awarded to a Kentucky Derby winner, so it wasn't like she didn't have enough flowers to work with. "I'll take care of this. Go ahead and start cleaning things up. The wedding starts in an hour."

Leon quickly gathered up all the discarded tissue paper that had been wrapped around the arrangements. She couldn't blame him for being eager to leave. "Anything else?"

"Maybe check with Mark to see if he needs help?" She nodded toward the offices turned dressing rooms on the far side of the lobby. "He should be delivering the bouquets by now."

"Yes, ma'am. Do you want me to go ahead and close up the van and move it?" He was looking toward the front doors, too, where a couple had just stepped in with an umbrella. "It's starting to rain."

"Sure." She watched him drop the wad of tissue onto the plastic drop cloth they'd put down to protect the carpet while they set up. He'd rolled up the plastic about halfway down the aisle when Robin realized something was off. "Wait." She counted off the sprays of roses and carnations decorating the end of each pew. "You said the van was empty?"

Leon's green eyes narrowed. He was getting defensive again. "Yeah?"

She pointed to the remaining rows of undecorated pews. "Where are the rest of my flowers? Does Mark have them in the back somewhere?"

"I can ask him."

"Never mind. You finish here and take care of the van. I'll find Mark."

Robin cursed the ticking clock and hurried down the aisle ahead of Leon. As soon as she stepped onto the marble tiles in the lobby, Jake moved from his post. He wrapped his hand around her elbow and pulled her away from the people coming in the front door.

"Are we done?" he asked. A couple of twentysomething women pointed to Jake, although he didn't seem to notice. But when one of them whispered the phrase, "Ghost Rescuer," his grip tightened and his shoulders expanded with a controlled breath. "I'm ready to leave anytime."

"Not yet." Robin pulled her arm from his grasp and searched the gathering crowd. "I promise I'm moving as fast as I can. I need to find my assistant."

"Bow-tie guy?"

Robin swung her gaze up at the apt description. "Yes. Mark. Have you seen him?"

He pointed to one of the two closed doors at the south end of the lobby. "Ladies' dressing room."

"Thanks." When Jake fell into step behind her, Robin turned and braced a hand at the center of his chest, offering him a wry smile. "*Ladies'* dressing room," she emphasized.

No wonder he was so eager to follow her. The two women weren't the only ones who'd noticed the big man dressed in jeans and a black T-shirt at the formal event. Robin observed at least two other groups chatting and pointing. Either they recognized Jake from that unfortunate picture in the newspaper this morning, or they were simply curious about why a man like him was attending a Kansas City society event. At least she'd convinced him to return his weapons out of sight beneath his pant leg, or else they'd really be talking. Or calling 911.

"Sorry about all this." She knew the spotlight was the last place where this man wanted to be. She gave him a way out for a few moments. "I left Emma sleeping up front. Do you mind getting her so she's not by herself?"

"Where will you be?"

"Tracking down someone who's not doing his job. Don't worry. I won't leave the church."

Robin dodged out of the way of flinging raindrops as a man in a pinstriped suit shook off his umbrella just inside the front door. Brian Elliott. Of course he'd show up at a gathering like this. Half his investment business was to see and be seen by Kansas City's wealthiest and most influential people. She recognized the woman with him as his executive assistant. Robin exchanged a polite wave and kept moving. She didn't need the kind of drama or delays Brian could bring into her life right now if she stopped for a conversation.

She'd been through two of the three carved-panel doors earlier in the day, helping the groomsmen pin on their boutonnieres and delivering the rosebuds Chloe Vanderham's hairdresser was pinning to her hair. Robin knocked on the last door, expecting to step inside to find gushing bridesmaids and Chloe's mother helping the bride get into her celebration gown.

Instead, she found three women in pink dresses and the mother of the bride standing in a circle around Mark Riggins, talking over each other as they looked at the pictures he was showing them on his phone.

"That's pretty."

"How about something for a dinner party?"

"All I need is the color palette or theme you want."

"I can get it for that price?"

"Mark?" Robin interrupted. "What are you doing? We're not finished in the sanctuary." She nosed her way in to Mark, dispersing the group. "Do you have the rest of those flower sprays?"

Mark shut down the internet connection on his phone, but not before she'd gotten a glimpse of the bouquet he'd been showing them. He tucked the phone into his shirt pocket and patted Robin on the shoulder. "Relax, boss lady. Chloe ordered twelve sprays of roses. I put up twelve sprays."

"I'm sure it was twelve down each side," she argued in a hushed voice.

"Twenty-four?" He shook his head, gently correcting her. "Your order said twelve."

No. Robin was certain that Chloe's ruby-red excess had demanded flowers on each and every pew. She knew she'd been distracted with the assault and subsequent threats, but she'd also been a successful businesswoman for several years now. Success didn't happen if she made costly mistakes like writing orders incorrectly.

Still, in front of the client wasn't the place to decide whether she was losing her business acumen—or whether she was losing *it,* period. Robin inhaled a deep breath and tugged Mark toward the door. "Then come help Leon clean up. The ushers are already out there, ready to seat people."

One of the attendants in pink stopped them on their way out the door. "Mark, do you have another card?" She hurried after them, waving a business card. "I can share them with my friends."

Business card?

"May I?" Robin borrowed the woman's card and read the decorative script. Mark Riggins: Affordable Flowers for Any Occasion. "What is this? This is your own website."

Mark glanced over his shoulder at the guests in the lobby and tried to push Robin back into the dressing room. "It's just a mockup of a card I designed."

Robin planted her feet in the doorway and held her ground. "You're working for me, but promoting your own business at a Robin's Nest Floral event? Oh, my God. You never talked to the distributor, did you? Have you been stealing my product and selling it as your own?"

Three pink ladies and a glaring Chloe Vanderham gathered to watch the confrontation.

"You're overreacting." Mark pulled his card from Robin's hand and handed it back to the attendant. "Can we have this discussion in private?"

"How is finding out that you've been stealing from me and my shop overreacting?"

With a noisy huff, Mark grabbed Robin's arm and dragged her into the empty office next door. "You're making a scene."

A public argument at an event like this wouldn't be good for her business, either. Robin shoved her fingers through her hair and paced across the small office to the edge of the desk there. "Please, Mark. We've been friends for a long time. Do you deny it?"

He locked the door and followed her to the desk without denying a thing. "It's not that big a deal. I've borrowed a few items from the stockroom. I had some successful events while you were gone with the baby. It's good publicity for your shop."

"No, it's good publicity for your online floral company."

"Well, clearly I can run the business without you. I'm ready to branch out."

"But you don't run the business." Robin had to put some space between them before she either smacked him or burst into tears at this betrayal. "You're not responsible for paychecks. You don't pay the bills. I do."

She barely heard the soft knock on the door. "Robin?"

"That's stealing, Mark." She looked up into those gentle features that had been a part of nearly every working day for almost a decade now. "It hurts me to say this, but I have to fire you."

He raised his hands in a placating gesture and closed the gap between them. "We can work together. Let me develop an online presence for you."

"No." She swatted his hands away when he grasped her shoulders. "How can I trust that you won't keep cheating me?"

A louder knock shook the door in the frame behind her. "Robin. Is everything all right?"

Jake. Of course, he'd be worried about her being out of his sight. "I'll be right out."

Angry color was creeping above the neck of Mark's bow tie. "Would you keep your voice down? We both have clients here."

Of all the nerve. Robin pointed two fingers at him. "You owe me at least two thousand dollars. Either you repay every cent or I'm going to press charges."

Mark snagged her wrist and squeezed it in his grip. "Press charges?"

"I'm giving you the option because of our friendship, but you know I'll do it." She tugged against his hold, but he wasn't letting go. "Do you know how stressed I've been with all the crazy stuff happening around me? I trusted that you were taking care of my shop when I couldn't be there. I thought you had my back."

"I wasn't hurting anybody."

The sharp crack of splintering wood spun them both around as the door swung into the room and Jake stepped inside. He looked from Robin to Mark, who instantly released his grip on her, and back to Robin. "Everything okay?"

Mark sputtered beside her. "You just broke a door in the church. Who's paying for that? Me, I suppose?" He tried to make a quick exit, but Jake was blocking the open doorway. He glanced over his shoulder at Robin and his slender shoulders sagged. "Add it to my tab."

It wasn't until she nodded that Jake stepped aside. "I'll have my lawyer contact you."

When Mark turned and walked out into the crowd of curious onlookers, Robin followed him to the door and clung to the splintered frame around the lock, scarcely aware of the organ music turning the guests' attention back to the sanctuary. She drew in a heavy breath, wishing she felt better about knowing the truth. "One mystery solved."

"Mark was cooking the books?" Jake came up behind her, cupping her shoulders. Robin leaned back against his solid strength. "Do you think he could have attacked you?" Jake asked against her ear. "Maybe to get you out of the way so he could recover any proof of his embezzlement?"

"I don't know. Mark doesn't seem like the violent type. Sneaky, yes—but swinging a baseball bat?" She turned when she could feel Jake stewing about something behind her. "What? Do *you* recognize Mark from the attack?"

"No, but…" *Answer the question, Jake. No more secrets, please.* He squeezed her hand where it rested against his chest. "Stay here."

"That's not an answer." The crowd parted as Jake moved through it. He caught up with Mark Riggins on his way out the side door to the street. Something Jake said—or maybe the hand clamped over Mark's shoulder—convinced him to turn around and come back into the office where Robin waited. "What are you doing?"

"Not a nice guy, remember?" Jake shoved Mark into the room, closed the door, then pushed Mark back against it, pinning him to the carved panels with a forearm pressed against his throat.

"Jake." She tugged at his arm, but it wasn't budging.

"What, you haven't humiliated me enough?" The forearm caught beneath Mark's chin and lifted him onto his toes. "Robin, call off your thug before he breaks my neck. That's going to leave a mark."

"I can do something worse if you don't answer my questions," Jake threatened. "Understand?"

Mark nodded.

"Jake?" Robin was more worried about Jake getting into trouble than Mark's comfort. "You said he didn't attack me."

"A few nights ago, I followed you around the corner from Robin's shop and saw you selling an envelope of photographs to a man wearing gloves."

"You followed me?" Jake's arm and Mark's common sense quickly silenced that protest. He nodded.

"What pictures?" Like those horrible threats she'd been receiving in the mail? Mark had something to do with that? She didn't know her friend at all, apparently.

"Who were those pictures of?" Jake prompted. "Robin?"

Mark glanced at Robin as his cheeks turned red from a dwindling oxygen supply.

"Tell him," she ordered.

"Emma. They were pictures of Emma. I'm so sorry."

"You sold pictures of my daughter?" Robin felt her own face heat up. She was livid. He got a break on cheating her business. But exploiting her daughter? "To some stranger?"

"Not lewd ones. Nothing illegal. Just pictures of her sleeping, or in her swing." Mark didn't seem to know whom he should be more afraid of. "The guy wanted them for his sister. She lost a baby and was really sad. He thought the pictures would cheer her up."

"What guy?" Jake demanded.

Another terrible thought had Robin turning about the room. "Where's Emma?"

"I left her with Shirley, the lady from your shop," he assured her before resuming the inquisition. "What guy?"

"I don't know his name. He came to the shop a couple of times while you were on maternity leave. Bought flowers. Paid cash. Left pretty quickly when he found out you weren't there." Mark's face was as red as the checks on his tie now. "I was getting the money to pay you back. To get some cash back into the accounts before you figured out what I was doing."

"Can you describe him?" Robin asked, as anxious to get eyes on her daughter as she was to find the truth. "The police can ask you these questions, too."

"I don't know. Brown hair. Business suit. Too buttoned-down and uptight for my tastes." Robin tugged on Jake's arm again, and this time he let Mark go. She grabbed Mark by the scruff of his starched collar herself and opened the door. She swept her gaze through the lobby, searching the line of waiting guests for one in particular. "There." She pointed to Brian Elliott, leaning down to hear a comment from his assistant. Mark knew Brian, didn't he? She'd dated Brian Elliott for almost two years before she'd broken it off. What other man in a suit showed up at her shop on a regular basis? "Is he the man you sold the pictures to?"

"No." With Jake flanking his other side, she didn't think Mark was lying. "Are you going to tell the police about this?" Mark dropped his voice to a pleading whisper after she released him. "Please. Yes, I was skimming business away from you—but I wouldn't do anything to hurt Emma."

Brian's questioning gaze found hers across the lobby,

but she quickly shook her head and turned away. She never answered Mark. She was deep in thought, thinking through all the men she knew. And how far too many of them, like every male guest here, wore business suits. Robin looked from acquaintance to acquaintance, from stranger to stranger, in the lobby, wondering if any man here had an interest in her and her daughter.

While she was distracted by wary suspicion and fear, Jake scooted Mark along his way toward the door again. "Get out of here. And if you're thinking of skipping town before you pay the lady back, I will find you."

Mark scuttled away, ignoring the curious looks and questions from the people he passed. He even blew off Leon when he stormed past him out the door.

Robin jumped at the brush of Jake's fingers against her back. "Now, can we go?"

She had a very bad feeling. Like the answer to whoever had threatened her was right here under her nose. Only she wasn't seeing the right picture. Only one thing would reassure her now. She spotted Shirley chatting with one of the ushers next to the table where Emma's carrier sat. "Emma?"

Jake guided her through the line of guests to the table set up beside the vestibule doors. "I'll get your coat and her bag. Be right back."

Robin thanked Shirley and dismissed her as Jake fetched their things. It almost made her smile to see that he'd set Emma's carrier on the Vanderhams' gift table. Emma truly was a gift in Robin's life, and the thought Mark taking pictures, of a stranger wanting to buy those pictures—of anyone wanting to separate Robin from the child who'd given her her first taste of true love—filled Robin's eyes with tears, instead.

But the smile won out when Emma saw her and squealed a happy laugh.

"Hey, sweetie. Are you watching all the people...?" Robin's voice trailed away when she saw the moisture on Emma's cheek. But Emma wasn't crying. Robin immediately wiped off the cool wetness. There was a smear of something on her pink-and-white blanket, too, as though someone with a dirty wet hand had touched it.

"Jake?" Her knees wobbled. Who had touched her baby? She looked back and forth. There were lots of people coming in from the rain with wet hands or moisture on their clothes. Who could resist that sweet face, sitting there and cooing, as the guests dropped off their gifts and cards and wandered past? Only, she had a feeling this wasn't some curious, cooing auntie who'd touched her child. "Jake?"

"What's wrong?" Jake draped her raincoat over her shoulders and positioned himself between Robin and the clamoring crowd.

"Ms. Carter?" a woman's voice called over the white noise of all the conversations in the crowded vestibule.

Robin ignored them all and lifted the soiled blanket away from her daughter. "Oh, my God." The breath seized up in her chest. Robin tossed the blanket aside and reached for the hand-sewn doll that had been tucked into the carrier with Emma.

"Where did that come from?"

Robin shook her head. "It isn't hers."

She picked up the doll. Like the blanket and Emma's cheek, it was soaking wet. Robin turned the unwanted gift in her hand. If she had found it in a craft store, she would have admired the even stitching and calico fabric. But everything about this gift was a vile incursion into her family, a threat that had literally touched her daughter. Who brought a doll to a wedding? This couldn't be accidental. "Who did this?"

She glanced up at Jake for answers, but he was searching the crowd, too.

"Ms. Carter?" Chloe Vanderham was pushing her way through the crowd.

When Robin saw the venom in her expression, she turned away from the impending confrontation. Her hand bumped against the carrier and the doll fell onto the table. The calico pinafore flipped up and Robin saw the name embroidered across the doll's chest.

Hailey.

"Robin?" Jake caught her when her knees buckled and wound his arm around her waist to keep her upright. "Stay with me. We'll figure this out."

"That's her birth name. Hailey is Emma's birth name. Bill Houseman—he said it was a matter of life or death that I talk to him." Robin's vision clouded over. She had to put her hands on Emma to make sure she was safe. "I never did."

Chloe Vanderham was upon them now. She drummed her ruby-red nails on the white tablecloth beside the baby carrier.

Robin didn't care that her client was unhappy. "Did you see who was with my daughter?"

"Are your people done?" Chloe wore a dressing gown over her long slip and petticoats. "The rain is already ruining my day, and all your drama is turning it into a disaster."

"I'm sorry, but this isn't her doll. There have been threats.... Did anyone see who gave it to her?" Robin looked all around, but now people seemed less interested in broken doors and spotting folk heroes from the newspaper, and more interested in getting away from the temperamental bride-to-be. Thunder rumbled overhead, punctuating Robin's disappointment. She splayed one hand over Emma's tummy and held on to Jake with the other. She wasn't going to find any more answers here today. She wasn't going to feel safe, either. "We're finished."

"Good. Now, please, both of you—" Chloe glanced down at Emma. "All of you—leave." She snapped her fingers and nodded to ushers in their black tuxedoes. "Get everyone seated. More guests are coming in. And tell Paul I'll be late coming down the aisle."

"I'm sorry. I…" But Chloe was already sweeping back into her dressing room with a huff. "Take me home, Jake." Robin reached for the vile doll. "I need to get Emma out of here."

"Wait. Don't touch it again."

"I'm throwing it away."

"Don't." He wrapped the doll up in the discarded blanket and closed his fist around it. He picked up the diaper bag that had fallen to the floor. "Do you have a plastic bag in here? The police may be able to get some kind of DNA off it."

Robin nodded. "Do we need to call KCPD? Or is it time I used Bill Houseman's card and ask him what he knows about this?"

"We'll send the cops after Houseman. Right now, I think we need to get out of here and find someplace friendlier and quieter where we can—"

"Talk things out?"

That firm mouth almost twisted with a grin. "Something like that. Let's go."

After bagging up the doll and blanket, Jake hiked the diaper bag onto his shoulder and cupped his hand beneath Robin's elbow while she covered Emma with a clean blanket and picked up the carrier. Robin was thanking a gentleman for holding the side door open for them when Jake pulled her back inside.

"What are you doing?"

"This way." He lengthened his stride, pushing a broad path through the guests in the lobby.

"But the SUV we rented is parked out back." Robin had to quicken her pace to keep up with him. "I don't mind a little rain."

"We're taking the scenic route."

"No, we're not." Robin tried to slow down, but he simply pulled her against his hip and cinched his arm around her to keep her moving at his speed. She was starting to learn how to read these sudden defensive maneuvers of his. "What did you see? What's happening?"

The rain hit her face and soaked through her hair to her scalp. Jake barely gave her time to pull the blanket over Emma's head before pulling the carrier from her grasp and hurrying them into a jog around the corner away from any main entrances.

"Jake," she protested as they crossed a gravel alleyway and entered the rear parking lot. "You're scaring me. I thought we agreed that you'd let me in on whatever's going on in that mind of yours."

"The empty place that can't remember anything? Or the scary part that thinks we're being followed."

"Followed?"

He punched the remote to unlock the car and set Emma in the backseat. "Get this thing attached."

With a soft curse, Robin moved in front of him and situated Emma in her car seat while Jake turned a slow 360 degrees behind her. She tried to steal a few glances around them, too, but saw no one. Just empty parked cars.

"Who's following us? Mark? I'd be happy to tell him he's fired again."

"It's not Riggins. It...may have nothing to do with you."

"What?"

"You get in, too." As soon as she finished, Jake pulled her back and shut the SUV's rear door. In the same fluid movement, he opened the passenger door and lifted her onto the seat. "I thought I recognized someone in front of the church."

Robin latched on to his hand before he could pull away. "You said you don't remember your past."

"Not that far back. Ever since that Ghost Rescuer stuff hit the papers, I keep seeing someone watching me. And I don't think he wants my autograph." He set the diaper bag in her lap. "Is your cell phone in there?"

"Yes." While she unzipped the bag and pulled her phone out, she tried not to let his vigilant sweep of the parking lot and streets beyond unnerve her too much. "Who is it? The Rose Red Rapist? Does he think you can stop him? Is it a reporter? The man Mark sold the pictures to?"

"I don't know." Once she had her phone in her lap, Jake dropped the car keys into her palm and curled her fingers around them.

Rain drops beaded on his face as he stood just outside the door and his icy eyes searched her face. "Jake?"

He brushed the damp hair off her cheek and tucked it behind her ear. "Just remember. I tried to be a good guy for you and Emma."

She turned her cheek into his palm. "You are."

He nodded, but she didn't think he looked like he believed what she did. When she opened her mouth to argue the point, he leaned in and kissed her. He stamped his possession on her lips and she gladly accepted the claim. The kiss was hard and brief, and filled with something more poignant than goodbye.

"Lock this tight and stay put," he ordered as he pulled away. "Call 911 if anything spooks you before I get back. If you don't see me in five minutes, drive to KCPD and show Montgomery the doll."

"If I don't see you…?" She reached for him, but he was already closing the door. "Where are you going?"

"To introduce myself."

Robin watched Jake head toward the corner of the building. The rain made dark stains on the shoulders of his T-shirt. He shifted his gun from his ankle holster to the back of his belt. He looked dangerous and determined and she wanted him back with her now. So she felt safe. So she knew he'd be safe, too.

Once he was out of sight, she checked her watch and marked the time. Five minutes.

What did he mean by *I tried to be a good guy for you and Emma*? Had he decided not to be a hero? What was he planning to do with that gun, anyway? Why was he kissing her goodbye?

She knew how to be alone. She knew how to take care of herself—and Emma. But that didn't mean she wanted to be alone. She'd opened up her heart to the secretive, wounded beast who was different from any other man she'd known. He was passionate. Protective. Moody. He could be gentle as a lamb or ferocious as a lion. She trusted him. She needed him. She might even love him.

No. There was no *might* about it. "He needs us, Emma," she whispered out loud. "And we need him."

Emma squealed her agreement.

But what kind of woman put her faith in a man who was so—?

"What the…?" She saw the young woman coming up

behind the SUV in the side-view mirror and the internal debate stopped. Strange. Despite all the cars parked around them, there wasn't another soul around. And suddenly this woman was here, standing in the rain when everyone else had dashed inside. Where had she come from? What did she want?

Robin's pulse kicked up a notch as the woman's sunken blue eyes locked on to hers in the mirror. There was something familiar about the dripping swing coat and straight dark hair. But she couldn't place her as one of the Vanderhams' guests. The woman touched her fingers to the rear fender of the SUV and trailed them along the wet black metal as she walked along its side.

Was she homeless? Had she been in accident?

"How do I know you?" Robin breathed. Even the rain falling around her seemed familiar. Outside the shop. The night of the assault. "That's it."

Recognition dawned, but brought little comfort. This was the same woman she'd seen watching the shop from across the street that night. Watching her. No. "Oh, God."

Watching Emma.

Robin scrambled to turn around in her seat. "Get away from my baby."

The woman stopped beside Emma's window. She smiled as she braced both hands against the glass and looked inside the vehicle. "Do you like your new toy? Mama made it just for you." Her eyes widened like saucers in her gaunt face. "Where is it? Where's your dolly?" Robin was on her knees, facing the woman when she smacked her palm against the glass. "What did you do with it?"

The sharp sound startled Emma, and after a beat of silence, she burst into tears.

With Robin temporarily forgotten, the woman tapped

on the window, trying to get Emma's attention. "No, baby. Stop crying." She felt all around the window, looking for a way to get in. "Baby? Don't cry."

"It's okay, sweetie." Robin reached over the back of the seat to take Emma's hand. But she only got louder and redder and more upset. "Back away from the car, please. You're frightening my daughter."

"That's my baby! You don't deserve her." Giving up on the window, the woman grabbed the door handle and rattled it. Thank God it was locked up tight. "I want my baby!"

When she reached for the front door handle, Robin leaned back and hit the horn. "Jake!" *Please come back.* She honked three more times and Emma's unhappiness grew louder. "It's okay, sweetie. We'll be okay."

"Hailey!" Emma's birth mother? The strange woman was a stranger no more. "Stop crying, baby."

Tania Houseman tried all the doors, rocking the SUV as she fought to get inside. Five minutes had passed. With the celebration in full swing inside, and the rain falling steadily outside, it seemed no one could hear Robin's pleas for help. "Leave us alone. You're not supposed to be here."

She pushed up higher in the seat to follow Tania's uneven walk as she staggered away from the car. Was she leaving? Was this freak encounter over? Robin lost sight of Tania for several precious seconds as she stooped down.

When she finally stood back up and turned toward the car, she held a fist-sized rock in her hand from the alley. "Hailey!"

Robin didn't think. She simply acted. She dove over the back of the seat and threw her body over Emma as Tania hurled the rock at the window.

The blow chipped the glass and Tania disappeared from sight again. While the disturbed young woman reloaded,

Robin unbuckled Emma from the car seat and pulled her into her arms. She hunkered down as close to the floor-boards as she could get, in case the window shattered. "Shh, sweetie."

Emma's cries filled the car as Robin flipped open phone and pressed 9.

"You should have died in that alley," Tania yelled. She pounded at the glass with another rock. "You don't de-serve her."

The glass splintered into a web of cracks and Robin pressed 1.

"I'm taking my baby." Tania raised the rock again.

A big black figure swooped up behind her, grabbed her arm and shook the rock loose. Robin whispered a grateful prayer as Jake twisted Tania's arm behind her back and pushed the woman's face up against the win-dow of the SUV.

"Is the kid okay?" Jake shouted through the glass.

Robin could only nod.

"Call Montgomery." Jake pulled Tania Houseman's coat down her arms, and twisted the sleeves to anchor her arms behind her. "I think we found your stalker."

Chapter Eleven

"You think her story's legit?" Detective Fensom asked.

"It'll be the biggest break we've had on our investigation yet if we can prove it's true." Spencer Montgomery never took his eyes off the glass. "Even if she IDs him, her testimony will never stand up in court."

"But we'd have DNA. With DNA and a reliable witness who can describe the attacks, we could put that bastard away."

Jake scrubbed his hand over his face and jaw and paced a circle around KCPD's Fourth Precinct observation room. The sun was setting outside. The rain still drummed on the rooftop. There were at least a dozen detectives and uniformed officers on the other side of that door in the building's third-floor bullpen.

And there was a man somewhere out there in the city who'd managed to track him to that church this afternoon.

No one had been able to track him for two years.

He'd spotted that retro-cool trilby hat, like that morning at the newsstand. Sitting in a car on the street in front of the church. With all the fancy trappings of that overblown soiree, he could bet that the driver with the black hat masking his face wasn't a guest. He could bet he wasn't on Jake's trail because he wanted a friendly family reunion, either. Who was that guy? DEA agent? Gun for hire? Someone with a personal grudge he couldn't remember?

After securing Robin and Emma in the car, he'd gone back to see what the guy's interest was in Jake's business. But the car was gone. Trilby guy was nowhere to be seen. And Robin had needed him.

Saving that woman was getting to be a regular habit.

But it was a job he needed to hand off to someone else.

His location in Kansas City had been compromised. If he wanted to stay alive, he needed to get out of this police station and get as far away from the responsibilities and unexpected notoriety of protecting a stubborn woman and her innocent child as he could get.

But he couldn't leave. Especially after hearing Tania Houseman's tragic story. His conscience wouldn't let him.

His heart wouldn't, either.

Jake felt trapped, caged like some sort of wild animal. He stood behind the mirrored window with Detectives Montgomery and Fensom and watched as Robin sat at the interview table in the adjoining room, trying to coax anything that made sense out of Tania Houseman.

Judgment day could come, and Jake knew he wouldn't leave Robin alone with the crazy woman who'd been identified as Emma's birth mother. If that whacko had gotten through the SUV's windows to Robin and Emma, Jake might be pacing a hospital corridor or even the morgue right now.

Whacko. Like he had room to talk. He took a deep breath and stopped at the window to watch Robin work some of that patient, stubborn magic that was changing him on the disturbed young woman who'd been calling, mailing and following Robin for weeks now, apparently. It was all part of Tania Houseman's obsession with the baby she'd given up for adoption.

A doctor from the Oak View Sanitarium sat in the room with her patient, after giving her whatever meds were necessary to calm her down. But it was Robin who'd finally gotten the woman talking after she'd either freaked out or shut down when the task force detectives had tried to interview her.

"When you're a mother, even when it's hard…you still have to be a mother." Robin had left Emma with Officer Wheeler in one of the nearby conference rooms. But she hadn't shied away from sitting down with the woman who'd butchered Emma's clothes and threatened to kidnap her. She sat at the table opposite the dazed young woman who scratched at the scars on her wrists. "I think you did a very brave thing by going through with the pregnancy after you'd been raped. You gave your daughter life, and I, for one, will always be grateful to you for that."

"I thought I could love her. I do love her." Tania lowered her gaze to the table. "I miss her."

"I know. I miss her terribly when I'm separated from her, too." Robin rubbed her hands up and down her arms, as if the temperature in the next room was dropping. She glanced back at the mirrored window and Jake moved toward her. Maybe she didn't need him right now. Maybe she was looking to the detectives for a bit of guidance on how to elicit the information they were hoping Tania could give. She turned back to the young woman across the table. "Tania, do you know who Emma's, I mean Hailey's, father is? Do you know who raped you?"

The younger woman, dressed in orange jail scrubs, nodded. "I never saw his face that night. But he gave me a red rose."

ROBIN PAUSED IN the doorway of the interview room as Dr. Freitag and a female police officer escorted Tania down the hallway to the restroom. She rubbed the weary tension in her neck and wondered if Emma was still asleep. She wished she was sleeping, too. Preferably with Jake's arms around her like they'd been last night so she could feel that sense of security his strength and warmth gave her. How did detectives like Spencer Montgomery and Nick Fensom do this kind of grueling, heart-wrenching work?

"Where's my sister?" Like everyone else on the floor, Robin turned at the man charging across the room from the sergeant's check-in desk. "Tania? Where are they taking her?"

Robin stepped forward to stop him and urge him to lower his voice. "To the restroom, Mr. Houseman. She'll be back."

The banking executive wore a suit and tie similar to the outfit he'd worn that day outside the Shamrock Bar when he'd warned her about a "life-or-death" problem. He was still preaching the same doom and gloom when he turned on Robin. "My sister is a sick woman. Whatever she's done, she isn't responsible."

Robin braced her hands at her hips. "Are you the responsible one in the family, then?"

"I tried to warn you. My sister is unstable. Who knows what she'll say or do?"

"She says she was assaulted by the Rose Red Rapist— that my daughter is the child of that rape."

That bold statement seemed to take him aback as much as seeing Spencer Montgomery, Nick Fensom and Jake step out of the adjoining room to form a semicircle around him. "This isn't about her vandalizing your car? Or sending those messages?"

"Or locking me in the refrigerator at my shop." Tania Houseman's misguided transgressions seemed minor, in retrospect, compared to what big brother had done. "She said you advised her not to report that she'd been raped."

Bill Houseman's hands went to the knot of his tie, needlessly straightening it. "I didn't find out about it until after the child was born."

"She's tried to kill herself at least once, judging by the scars on her wrists. She needs to talk to someone about it."

As the circle of armed men closed in around him, Bill Houseman grew more agitated. "I did what I thought was right. At first I thought she was less than thrilled about having a baby because she had just launched her art career with her first big show." He raked his fingers through his perfectly styled hair and left a rumpled mess in their wake. "About halfway through the pregnancy, she changed. She became sullen, depressed. She stopped painting. That's when I sent her to the Oak View Sanitarium. She had the baby and came home and was happy for a month or so. Then she woke up one morning and slit her wrists." He turned to share his explanation with Jake and the detectives. But he wasn't finding much sympathy there, either. "That's when she told me about the rape. I had her sign away her rights and put Hailey up for adoption. I wanted to get any symbol of that monster out of Tania's life."

Jake stepped forward to defend Emma before Robin could. "There's no monster in that little girl. She's a beautiful, perfect baby."

"I thought maybe getting that baby back would bring Tania back to me. It's not easy to watch the talented little sister you grew up with waste away into an empty-eyed shell of herself."

"That's why you attacked me?" Robin asked. "Was Tania trying to kidnap my daughter while you dragged me into that alley?"

"No. That was all on me. I thought I'd knocked you out,

and I was going to take the baby then. But you wouldn't stay down."

Spencer Montgomery had an idea on that. "So you tried to make it look like a rape so that we'd look for a different type of suspect. Not someone trying to kidnap a child."

"I just wanted my sister to be happy again."

"Billy?" Tania, barely vocal, shuffled a little faster down the hall as she went to greet her brother.

Bill Houseman wound his arms around her slender shoulders and pressed a kiss to the crown of her hair. "Hey, kiddo. How are you holding up?"

"Better. The police department has a victim specialist I can talk to." She glanced back at the woman behind her. "And Dr. Freitag says the hospital has a trauma-recovery program I can go to. Is that all right?"

"Whatever you need." Billy gave his sister another kiss and then handed her back to the doctor. "Take good care of her."

Dr. Freitag put a supportive arm around her patient to lead her down the hallway. But the fragile young woman who'd endured far more than she should stopped and turned to her brother. "It's better for Hailey—" she flashed an apology to Robin "—for Emma, I mean—to be with Ms. Carter. She loves her, too."

Billy nodded and winked at his sister. Once Tania and the doctor had left the floor, Houseman turned to Detective Montgomery, who must have been exuding enough authority that he assumed, correctly, that Montgomery was the man in charge. "Are you pressing charges against my sister?"

"That's up to Ms. Carter."

Robin shook her head. "Your motives might be in the right place, Mr. Houseman. Your methods, however, are unforgivable."

Bill Houseman nodded. "You can't prove I've done anything. We're just having a friendly conversation here. You never Mirandized me."

Jake moved to stand beside Emma and draped an arm around her shoulders. "Ask him if he still has a bruise under his collar from where I put a choke hold on him that night. From what I hear, it leaves a mark."

Nick Fensom looked like he was ready to rip open Bill's collar on the spot. "Well, Mr. Houseman?"

Houseman was fiddling with his tie again. "I think I'd like to talk to my attorney now."

JAKE WAITED FOR Nick Fensom to escort Bill Houseman to lockup before he went down to the conference room where Robin had given Emma a bottle and was changing her. The hour was late, he was bone tired and he needed a shave. But when he looked into the room and saw how Robin's face lit up as she played a tickle game with her daughter, and heard how Emma's laughter filled the room, he smiled.

The moment didn't last, though. Spencer Montgomery walked up beside him. He pulled back the front of his suit coat and stuck his hands into his pockets. But Jake didn't believe there was anything casual about the detective's thoughts and actions.

"We need to verify Ms. Houseman's statement," he started, without any preamble, "but the MO she described of her assault matches what other victims have said about the Rose Red Rapist, including some details we've never released to the public." Montgomery watched the mother and daughter show for a few seconds before adding, "If our unsub finds out that baby is his—that we now have his DNA—"

"Then he'll go after Emma." Jake glanced over at the

detective. "Let's try to keep that particular story out of the newspapers, okay?"

"Agreed. Ms. Carter has already agreed to let our lab take blood samples from her daughter. Do you think she's figured out what kind of danger they'll be in?"

"The woman is too smart not to."

Jake had been thinking a lot about Robin and Emma's chances for a happily ever after if he saved his own hide and left K.C. He'd also been thinking about his own chance at happiness if he left the Carter girls behind and someone even more violent than a disturbed young woman and her misguided brother hurt them.

Talk about a guilty conscience.

"Are you staying on as bodyguard?"

"I'm not going anywhere," Jake vowed.

Montgomery nodded. "Agent Nash stopped by my office this afternoon. I sent him to the *Journal* to talk to Gabe Knight about those articles he wrote on you. He's going to call me later tonight. Are you still unavailable?"

Jake was wondering if his instinct to trust Spencer Montgomery was a smart one, or just wishful thinking. "Did this Agent Nash say anything about me?"

"He showed me a picture of you—when you were younger and prettier." Good one. Jake almost laughed. "He said he's your handler."

"Handler?" Jake looked the detective straight in the eye. Nash hadn't come with a wanted poster?

"He said you were one of the best undercover operatives he's ever worked with. Apparently, you've been listed as MIA for a couple of years now. What happened? Did you go AWOL on a mission?"

He was one of the good guys? That DEA badge in his pocket was his? Then who did he kill? And why was the guy in the trilby hat following him? It was a lot of information to process. And he had no way of knowing how much or little of that information was true until he talked to Nash or the mystery guy in the hat.

"It's a long story." Reenergized by the need to verify some answers and possibly get a breakthrough to his missing past, Jake nodded to the detective and headed into the conference room to gather the Carter girls and their things.

"I drink coffee and bourbon," Montgomery called after him. "Stick around town at least until my task force catches its man, and I'll buy you a drink and listen to that story."

A few minutes later, Jake was in the Fourth Precinct parking garage, keeping watch while Robin buckled in the car seat. Her movements weren't as efficient as usual and that worried Jake. "Tired?" he asked.

At first Robin shook her head. "Yes, but..."

But that wasn't what was bugging her.

"What is it?"

"Look at how that assault affected Tania Houseman, and the terrible things her brother did because of it." She pulled a blanket up over Emma and tucked it beneath her chin. Her hand lingered at Emma's round cheek. "If he is her father, if Emma is the product of a brutal rape—will she ever have to find out?"

Jake wrapped his arm around her and pulled her close, pressing a kiss to her temple. He reached inside the SUV and lay his hand over Robin's to cup Emma's cheek. "A person can handle anything if she has love and support in her life." A hell of a lot better than by isolating oneself from the world, he was learning.

"She's got you to protect her, right?" Robin nestled her head beneath Jake's chin and an unexpected warmth filled his chest.

Was this thing real between them? Or was a real relationship, a real family, ever in the cards for a man like him?

"No, honey. She's got you. She can't have a stronger, stauncher ally than her mother."

JAKE KNEW SOMETHING was wrong as soon as he turned onto the long gravel driveway. Even with the moonless sky and drizzle of rain misting the air, there should be some light beyond the SUV's high beam headlamps to guide their path. But there was no yard lamp, no security lights, no night-light burning through the kitchen window.

"Power's out."

Robin roused herself from where she'd been dozing against the headrest and sat up straight. "I didn't think the storm was that bad. What time is it?"

"After midnight."

She pushed the tumbled waves off her face and scanned the countryside with him. "I can't even see the barn, much less the trees behind it."

"Or what's over the next hill on either side of the road."

He checked the rearview mirror when she looked in the backseat to ensure that Emma was still sleeping. "I've got flashlights in the kitchen and bedroom, and camping lanterns in the basement."

Jake nodded, wishing he could believe that a lightning strike had taken out a local transformer. But he'd been in survival mode for too long to not be suspicious. "I've got a flashlight in my go-bag, too." Instead of pulling around to the garage behind the house, Jake stopped at the side-walk leading up to the front door. "Let's get the kid out and put to bed first, and then I'll go downstairs to double-check that we haven't thrown a breaker."

Leaving the headlights on to light their path, they un-loaded Emma in record time and dashed up to the porch before they got too wet. Jake peered into the darkness for any signs of movement while Emma pulled out her keys to unlock the door.

"Jake?" He turned around to see the front door floating open. Robin's key was still in her hand. "I never forget to lock it."

"Stay behind me." Something was definitely wrong. And it wasn't any power outage.

He pulled his Beretta from its ankle holster and nudged the door open. He sniffed the air and picked up a faint scent that was neither perfume nor baby powder. No, this one was more tobacco and man sweat.

Maybe she smelled it, too. "I've had a break-in?" she whispered.

"Looks like it." With one hand clutching the back of his shirt and the other holding Emma's carrier between them, Robin followed Jake through the living room into the kitchen. There were no other signs of broken windows or forced locks. Her CD stereo system was still on its shelf; a small television sat on the kitchen counter. "It's not a robbery."

"Then what? Someone getting out of the rain?" They paused for her to get a flashlight and hand it to Jake. Crossing the gun and flashlight at his wrists, Jake led a quick search through the rest of the main floor, ending up in the family room, where the quilt from this morning still lay in a clump at one end of the sofa. "I thought these threats against Emma and me were done."

"They are. The Housemans aren't going to bother you anymore." His stomach fisted in his gut. "This is about me. I'm sorry, honey. I think my nightmare followed me here."

She moved up beside him. "How do you know?"

"That." He pointed the beam of the flashlight at the square coffee table and heard her gasp.

Jake's fake passports and IDs were spread neatly across the top of the coffee table. In the middle of them all, the intruder had carved a symbol into the dark wood and jammed the knife he'd most likely used into the middle of it.

Robin's fingers pinched into his forearm. "What does that mean?"

Jake didn't know, but he had a feeling the capital *G* with all the extra curlicues wasn't anything good. "Give me the kid." He hoisted the carrier in one hand and nodded to the front door. "Let's get out of here."

The red targeting laser dotted Robin's chest and he had no time to do more than to shove her out of the way before the front window shattered and a white-hot poker ripped through his left shoulder.

"Jake!"

The impact of the bullet knocked him back across the table. "Get down!"

A trio of shots peppered the brick fireplace, spraying chips of shrapnel across the room. He heard the reports a split second later and tried to gauge the distance of the shooter, but three more shots zinged over his head before he could crawl back to the sofa to kill the flashlight and pull Robin and Emma down to the floor beneath him.

"You're bleeding."

They were all going to be bleeding soon if he couldn't get a bead on this guy and take him out. "It went through. That's better than having the bullet inside."

He felt Robin's cool hand at the scar on his temple an instant before he felt the pain webbing through his shoulder. "Ow!"

"Sorry. No, I'm not. Not really." She'd dumped Emma's bag and was pressing a diaper against the wound to stanch the bleeding. Oh, yeah, this one was smart. But tending to the injured wasn't going to keep them alive over these next few minutes. He checked the magazine in his gun and the one in his pocket. Thirty shots. The shooter had already fired off at least half that number.

Right now their best move was the phone, not more guns. He dug Robin's cell out of the mess on the floor and thrust it into her hands. The diaper fell and warm blood trickled down his arm again. "Call Montgomery for backup."

Six more shots. He palmed the top of Robin's head and pulled her into his chest to shield her as chunks of wood and plaster rained down on them.

Jake's go-bag was missing. That meant whoever was out there was armed to the teeth. And judging by the message on the coffee table, he knew how to use any weapon Jake could.

"Can you take a picture with that phone?"

"Yes?"

"Send a picture of that carving to Montgomery. Tell him to show it to Agent Nash to see if it means anything to him."

Robin nodded and raised the phone to capture the image. Jake pushed up from his position to fire three random shots to give her some cover. "Got it."

"Texts only. I don't want any phone ringing to give our position away."

"Who's Agent Nash?" Robin huddled back against his chest and sent the text. "What's going on? Who are those people?"

"It's just one guy. Somebody like me."

"Who is Agent Nash?"

"Robin, you know all that talking you like me to do?" The laser-targeting light swung away and Jake saw their chance to move to a more secure location. He pushed the carrier into Robin's hands and pulled her to her feet, urging her to keep low as they ran toward the back door. "It's going to have to wait until later."

A flash-bang grenade lit up the room they'd just vacated. Someday, he'd think about how angry it made him to think the place where he'd first made love to Robin was now burning. But right now, Jake could only think about getting them all to safety. "He can't find us in the house. Let's move."

A second flash-bang hit the kitchen and startled Emma into a screeching panic. Jake opened the back door and pulled Robin along the side of the house behind him. "If we can get to the barn, you and Emma can hide out inside the wall of hay bales. That should give you a little more protection."

"You're coming with us." Robin accidentally tugged on his wounded arm and Jake cursed.

"I'll get you to the barn."

Their attacker had found Jake's semi-auto and was cutting a line of bullet holes through the front room now. With every new loud sound, Emma cried out. "Can you keep her quiet? Hiding won't do us any good if her crying gives us away."

Robin pulled Emma from her carrier to hug her right up against her chest. "Shh, sweetie. Mommy needs you to quiet down."

A knot of dread formed in Jake's stomach as nightmare and reality blended together. Darkness. Burning. Explosions. Somebody wanted him dead.

"Jake?" Robin's touch startled him and he looked over the jut of his shoulder at her. "Stay with me. Don't go to that place. Here."

She placed Emma into the crook of his good arm.

"Feel the rain? It's cool." Another burst of gunfire made

him jump. "Listen to Emma. See?" The infant's shrieks had quieted to a few intermittent sobs. Robin stroked her hand across his brow and quieted the nightmare. "Are you with me?"

Squeezing the haunting images from his mind, he looked down into her sweet, gray-blue eyes and nodded. "Honey, I'm supposed to save you."

A flash-bang detonated in the bedroom behind them and all three of them jumped. "I think you'll still get your chance."

He hugged Emma as close to his chest as he dared. "Stay low to the ground. And run."

Once he had Robin and Emma secured behind triple hay bale stacks in the barn, Jake pulled out his half-spent Beretta. "You know how to use a gun?"

"No."

He placed the gun into Robin's hands and gave the quickest lesson of his life. "Safety's off. Squeeze the trigger—don't jerk it. And don't shoot me."

She grabbed hold of him, curling her fingertips into his chest. "Where are you going? Backup's coming, isn't it?"

"Maybe not soon enough. If this guy's like me, only one of us is getting out of here alive." Her skin paled and Jake leaned in and kissed her. This is who he was, who she needed him to be. "I intend it to be me."

"I love you," she whispered as he pulled away.

Jake nodded and kissed her again.

The lights of the approaching sirens finally diverted their attacker's attention away from the house. With the rain muffling his footsteps, Jake snuck up on the man's flank. The light wasn't good, but it didn't have to be at this distance.

Jake pulled his knife and flipped it in his hand. And when the perp in the trilby hat finally realized he wasn't alone, he swung around with the semi-automatic. But Jake was quicker.

Twenty seconds later he was standing over a dead man with a knife stuck in his heart. Robin and Emma were finally, truly safe.

He kicked the stupid hat aside and looked back toward the barn. "I love you, too."

Chapter Twelve

"Joe! Hey, Joe!"

Jake looked up from the baby cooing in his lap on the gurney where a pair of EMTs had bandaged the through-and-through in his shoulder. The guy, blond-haired and long-legged, was chasing the ambulance in his jeans and cowboy boots, trying to catch it before the doors closed and they drove him away for a routine check and some stitches in the E.R.

The man wasn't much older than Jake, but the badge and sidearm on his belt demanded that he didn't just blow him off for a private ride with the Carter girls and, he hoped, one of those conversations that Robin liked.

"Detective Montgomery said you'd been avoiding me. If you aren't the cagiest son of a gun to track down. The rest of the squad thought you were dead."

Robin got up from the side bench and sat on the edge of the gurney beside Jake. Did she think he was in trouble with this cop? He grinned at how protective a mother could be, even with someone who didn't need protecting. "Who are you?"

"Ma'am." He extended his hand to introduce himself. "I'm Nash. Agent Charles Nash. DEA." He pulled his badge off his belt to show her, and she passed it along to Jake. Hell. He sat back a little. It looked just like the badge he'd kept all this time—with a different name, of course. When Jake returned the badge to the officer, he made a face. "It's Charlie. Your handler?"

"Charles Nash?" Jake repeated, waiting for some sort of recognition to kick in. "I work for you?"

"Yeah, Joe. What kind of game are you playing?" Agent Nash snapped his fingers at whatever revelation he was about to share. "Oh, man. I knew you'd been hit, but I had no idea it affected your memory."

"You know me?"

"Yeah. Joseph Lonergan. DEA agent. Best undercover man I ever worked with." He climbed up into the ambulance to take the seat Robin had vacated. "We lost you on a mission to Tenebrosa. You infiltrated Diego Graciela's cartel. Killed the don yourself to save some girls he'd kidnapped to use as prostitutes. Blew your cover, of course. I tried to pull you out. But the compound got leveled by a rival cartel's truck bomb, and the agency assumed you were dead."

Explosions. Heat raining down. The nightmare *was* a real memory.

"I didn't give up on you, though. I know how resourceful you are. I figured if there wasn't a body, then you'd gone underground. I've been looking for you ever since. Thought I'd warn you about the hit Graciela's brother put out on you." He pointed out the door to the coroner's wagon that was hauling away the shooter KCPD had identified as Johnny Cortez. "The symbol carved into this lady's coffee table was Graciela's—I'm sure that was a message from the brother. But I gather you already figured that out."

Unfortunately, Jake followed the information about the cartel and hit man better than a couple of other things. "I'm Joe Lonergan?"

"He goes by Jake now," Robin volunteered.

"Your head really is scrambled, isn't it?" The perpetual grin faded from Nash's expression. "So no memory of killing Graciela or feeding us enough intel to close down his pipeline into the U.S.?"

Jake shook his head. "The doctors say my memory may never return."

Agent Nash nodded. "I'll send you copies of the mission briefings and your reports up until the day we lost contact. You can read up and see what a pain you were—and see all the good work you got done for us."

"Thanks." Jake laced his fingers together with Robin's. "So I'm a good guy, after all. Is that a deal breaker?"

She tightened her fingers around his. "What deal are you talking about?"

Whatever Nash was to Jake—boss, friend, coworker—he was a little slow about picking up the signals that Jake wanted some time alone with this very brave, very special woman.

"Your job's waiting for you if you want to come back," Nash offered.

Jake nodded his appreciation. "I'll need some time to think about it. My brain has a lot of catching up to do."

And he knew he wouldn't be leaving K.C. until the potential threat to Robin and Emma was resolved and the Rose Red Rapist case was finally closed.

Agent Nash shook hands with Jake and stood. "Take whatever time you need. But we'll keep in touch this time. No more going into hiding and covering your tracks. Come see me in Houston. And I'll check in next time I'm in Kansas City. Ma'am." He nodded to Robin. He tapped his finger against Emma's nose and she giggled. "Cutie." Then he was hopping off the ambulance. "Take care. If you need anything, call."

"Agent Nash?"

He turned. "It's just Nash. Or Charlie if we've been drinking."

Jake nodded. Nash. Still not ringing a bell, but it was hard not to like the guy. "Can you answer a question for me?"

"Anything."

"Am I married? Do I have kids?"

Nash shook his head. "Your philosophy was that the work you did was too dangerous to have any kind of family. Your parents are both gone. You've got no siblings—some cousins and an aunt in San Antonio, I think. But that's one of the reasons you volunteered for the long-term deep-cover op. You were a free man."

Jake tunneled his fingers into the silky waves at Robin's temple. "Not anymore." He couldn't take his gaze away from those pretty eyes that seemed to like looking at him. "Thanks for finding me, Nash."

"Yeah, well next time you get shot in the head, don't make it so hard to track you down."

Nash left and Jake scooted forward on the gurney, slipping his good arm around Robin's waist and pulling her closer. "I don't want to be a free man. I want connections. I want to be tied to a home and a family."

She lay her hand against his scarred face. "Anyone in particular?"

"The Carter girls. If they'll have me. I happen to have fallen in love with both of them."

"All right, Joe."

He frowned. That didn't sound right. "Call me Jake."

"Okay. Jake."

He pulled her up to his chest and covered her mouth with his, claiming her lips, claiming her heart, claiming this family. They traded a dozen more kisses, some hard and fast, others sensual and lingering, and still others that were gentle and healing and perfect.

The doors closed and the ambulance shifted into gear. Jake settled both the Carter girls into his arms. He was dozing off toward a peaceful sleep when he realized the unthinkable and sat up. "Hey. Did I just win an argument?"

* * * * *

Look for the next book in USA Today
bestselling author Julie Miller's miniseries
THE PRECINCT: TASK FORCE, *on sale September
2013 wherever Harlequin Intrigue books are sold!*